ULTRA VIOLET

AIDA SALAZAR

SCHOLASTIC PRESS

NEW YORK

Library of Congress Cataloging-in-Publication Data
Names: Salazar, Aida, author.
Title: Ultraviolet / by Aida Salazar.
Description: First edition. | New York : Scholastic Press, 2024.
| Audience: Ages 10 and up. | Audience: Grades 7-9. | Summary: Thirteen-year-old Elio is struggling
with "coming of age"—first love, first heartbreak, first real fight (which lands him in the hospital),
and what it means to be a "man," a true friend, and an ally, as well as
how to overcome a culture of toxic masculinity.

Identifiers: LCCN 2023003274 (print) | LCCN 2023003275 (ebook)
| ISBN 9781338775655 (hardcover) | ISBN 9781339027432 (ebook)
Subjects: LCSH: Mexican American boys—Juvenile fiction. | Machismo—Juvenile fiction.
| Masculinity—Juvenile fiction. | Interpersonal relations—Juvenile fiction. | Emotions—
Juvenile fiction. | CYAC: Novels in verse. | Mexican Americans—Fiction. | Machismo—
Fiction. | Interpersonal relations—Fiction. | Coming of age—Fiction.
| LCGFT: Bildungsromans. | Novels in verse.

Classification: LCC PZ7.5.S23 Ul 2024 (print) | LCC PZ7.5.S23 (ebook) |
DDC 813.6 [Fic] —dc23/eng/20230314 LC record available at https://lccn.loc.gov/2023003274 LC ebook
record available at https://lccn.loc.gov/2023003275

10 9 8 7 6 5 4 3 2 1   24 25 26 27 28
Printed in Italy   183
First edition, April 2024
Book design by Marijka Kostiw

For my

sun, João,

and your

tender

ultraviolet

heart.

Ultraviolet

Who invented love, anyway?
Had to be a girl, right?
    Had to be.
'Cause I don't get it.

Who can understand
the feeling of shimmering sol
that swallows anything smart
you wanna say
and tangles your blushing nerves
up inside your growling guts
    so bad,
    you almost wanna fart
    so bad,
    your skin turns all goose bumpy?

Just by looking at the
brown besos of her eyes,
the embers of her cheeks,
hearing the sound of her voice in the key of F
    entering your ears,
    taking root inside
the blob of your thirteen-year-old dude brain

and washing everything you see
with a reel of colors
beyond the spectrum
>red,
>
>orange,
>
>yellow,
>
>green,
>
>blue,
>
>indigo,
>
>violet.

More than that.

>Ultraviolet.

Glow-in-the-dark outrageous.

It's what I see

when Camelia is around.

Is this what it feels like to be

in love?

Irrational Fears

Bees.
Abejas scare me rotten.

There, I said it.

I know. Of all the things
I could be afraid of, like

> El Cucuy
> the plague
> earthquakes
> La Llorona
> fires.

It's bees.
Tiny, hurt-nobody bees.

It's the worst when a critter zooms by
because I lose all sense and wild jiggle
my whole body so it won't sting me.

No, the worst is
when I'm around my boy, Paco.

Closest friend I have
my bud, my dude,
my "I got your back" kinda bro,
and a bee zim zams near me
forcing me to do the wild jiggle and run
'cause he laughs at me,
calls me a miedoso.
Stone-cold scaredy-cat.
And I have to hold myself back
from punching him on the arm
for him to quit it.

Just the thought
takes me right to the time I was six
swinging on the monkey bars.
I smashed a bee with my hand
against the metal.
I jumped off, my hand shooting streaks
of pain, turning on the siren of my wail
fire-engine red blasting through my boca.
It made Moms stop pushing my little sisters
on the swings and come running to me
with a

      ¿Qué pasa, Elio? ¿Mi'jo?

zigzagging
across her face.

My throbbing hand swelling,
my lips turning blue,
the weighted blow of pain
pulling me down to the ground
at Moms's feet until
my face hit the sand.
Passed out. Stone-cold. Frío.

Then waking up a second later
just to keep crying
and pushing sand off my tongue
and Moms crying to see I'd come to,
and my sisters crying to see Moms crying,
my heart pounding louder than our cries,
all of us looking like a broken walnut—
tight, brown, and crumbled together.

The world spun so much I couldn't see
the blue clouds and white sky
turn that moment into
what my pops calls an "irrational fear"
which I can't get over

no matter what I do
to erase it.

Yeah, bees.

And my body growing
explosively like an Animorph
leaving purple Wolverine
stretch mark scratches
on my back and butt.

Puberty.
Wild and scary stuff.

And girls.
I used to be afraid of girls
until I met Camelia.

Knock Out

Eighth grade at
RISE UP STEM to STEAM Middle School
rolled around and everyone was coupling up.
Straight, gay, nonbinary, trans, artist kids,
STEM kids, band kids—didn't matter.
The hormones were poppin'
I mean, everyone was down bad!

> Joaquin and Teresita
> Amanda and Christina
> Mar and Azul
> Danny and Juan.

Paco basically yelled as he pounced
on my shoulders while we walked
through the front doors of school.

> *Bro, it's the first week of eighth grade!*
> *Why is this even happening?*

But that didn't stop him.
Paco got to work scanning the halls
and before I knew it, he was chatting up Laurette
the güerita whose family is from Chihuahua.

A big cheesy grin and round eyes poppin' outta
his mosquita muerta reddish-brown face.
Silly stupid happy.
No idea how he even learned
those moves.

Not me, I didn't go looking.
I was too scared.

All this love stuff smacked me
                on the jaw
                        like a good right hook
                and knocked
                me
                out.

Straight Frozen

I was seriously minding my business.
I had just left my locker
with the machaca burrito
Pops packed for lunch
and was walking into the cafeteria
when I felt it.

      The pull of watching eyes.

Sounds creepy, I know,
but it was less skin-crawly
and more, I don't know, magnetic.

So obviously, I turned my sweaty head
      and there she was

           a girl with a blue streak
           running through the front
           of her short brown hair
           with honey-hazel skin
           and a face so bright and round
           it looked like a gigantic sunflower
           just staring.

She smiled at me and I froze
        right in my tracks.
        I wasn't entirely sure if it was me
        she was smiling at
        but in case it was
        I wasn't going to move.

I mean, I couldn't.
I didn't even register Paco
who came barreling toward me asking,

        So, you gonna split that machaca burrito with me
        or what?

I was straight frozen.
        Like freeze-tag frozen.

If it hadn't been for Paco
seeing how spaced out I was
and shoving me so hard
        I crashed into a kid walking by,
I probably would still be there
completely helado.

Camelia in the Light

Camelia was sitting
at the artsy-fartsy lunch table
where all the visual arts kids sit
holding a pencil
and an oversized sketchbook on her lap,
a yellow glow of light
bursting behind her.

My mind went racing
through all the possibilities.
    Was she sketching me?
    Was I annoying her?
    Was this actually a stink eye?
    Or was she just looking
    beyond me
    at the disheveled crop of
engineering and musician kids
sitting where I usually sit?

Then, she smiled.
It was one of those
    too-good-to-be-true
    sparkle-on-the-teeth

kind of smiles too.
Sunrays and everything.

I think my jaw
          dropped open
because I was absolutely certain
she   *was*   smiling at me.

She couldn't have been smiling at Paco,
who had his back to her
clueless that she was even there
and who by this time
          was jumping all over me
          stealing my burrito and laughing
with our friends—Luisito, Cheo, and Raul.

Camelia's shining smile
was all the fuel I needed
          to shoot him off me
and smile back.
Then, clearly still under her spell,
          I made a beeline
          for the open seat
          right next to her.

Paco, Luisito, Cheo, and Raul
were yelling and trailing behind me:

> *Ooh, watch out, now!*
> *Get to steppin'!*
> *Scared of you!*
> *Dale gas, fool!*

It was steel-band loud.
Kaleidoscopic colors bounced
off the walls
but somehow, somehow,
      the swirl of my world
settled into one
finite focal point
of glimmering quiet,
    her
    sweet
    sunflower
    face.

I may have tripped over
the first words
I ever said to her,

Uh, what are you drawing?

This manga called Witch Hat Atelier. *You wanna
see?*

I answered with an idiotic,
Nice!

I peeked over her shoulder
to see she was a really good drawer.
Like super talented
and all that.

I heard someone snicker.
It was a broody, skinny kid
        named Chava
sitting at the artsy-fartsy table
across from her.
Whatever.

Then she smiled again
and literally
my heart
shot out my chest
like an out-of-control

boomerang
and zoomed back
in three seconds.

No one ever explained
something so out of this world
could happen to me

and that one of those
      hard-to-erase
      irrational fears
would disappear

into the flash
of all her light.

So Alike

Camelia is hella cool.
Like supremely beautiful and strange
in all the best ways.

I looked it up and it turns out,
she's named after
      a flower
      and it shows.
A camellia is so strong
it takes two weeks to wilt when cut.

With Camelia everything is real.
The like-her-a-lot kinda feelings.
The maybe-it's-love kinda feelings.
Ultraviolet feelings
      that juke around my body
      that turn on places in me
      I didn't know existed.

We marathon text after school
for three days straight
and I can confirm she is "the one"
based on these facts:

she prefers Marvel over DC

like me,

she's done martial arts

like me,

she's into hip-hop musicals

like me,

she takes no one's mess,
well, except for the bees,

so sorta like me,

and she draws manga and anime
my absolute freakin' favorite.

She can't be more perfect.
She can't.

Well, maybe if she played piano
like me,

but whatever,
she's near perfection.

I wonder if the world has
turned ultraviolet
for her too?

I almost ask her
but then
I think twice.

Whoever heard of having your whole vision
change because you met some girl?

Except she isn't some girl.

She is Camelia
whose flower name
makes it rain
ultraviolet.

You Wanna Go Around?

Maybe it's how
beauti-licious Camelia is
      that makes any fears
                scoot away.

    Maybe it's
    the colors that fire off
    when I see her.

    Maybe because
    I practiced a thousand times
    in the mirror . . .

I dunno.

But something
      swishing and swirling
around
      inside me
      gives me the guts

to walk right up
to Camelia's artsy-fartsy table

today, on the fourth day of liking her,
pull her aside so we could be alone,
and ask her the question
I was hearing everyone
else asking the kids they liked . . .

Camelia, you wanna go around?

Huh? Around what?

She hadn't gotten the memo. Oof.

I feel like a flaming
chicharrón all deep-fried and flaky.

You know, like go around, together?

You've lost me, Elio.

Camelia's eyelids fall
like blinds
halfway down
a window.

I mean, I mean . . . would you like to be my girlfriend?

Ohhhh! That's what that is? Um, yeah! I would!
she says, nodding wildly.

Then, she wraps
her arms
around
my neck
and squeeeezes me
so tightly
        she chokes
                the chicharrón
                        right out of me.

The Firsts

That's when I realize
I *am* her boyfriend,
not just any boyfriend,
but her first
and she's my first girlfriend.

It makes my heart
pound like a jackhammer
so much, it kinda hurts.

The happiest
and sappiest
I've ever been.

Sucka Bump

I'm dazed and drenched
in ultraviolet as the bell rings
and I start to walk away from Camelia,
when that kid, Chava,
bumps into me so hard,
he almost throws me off
my happy axis.

¡Órale! I shout.

Watch where you're going, bean pole! he says.

Chava doesn't even look at me
but locks his eyes on Camelia
and keeps on going.

Normally, those'd be fighting words
but I shrug them off 'cause Camelia
is pumping through my veins.
I'm feeling so fresh, flowing, charged,
I could do wild backflips
down the hall.

But on second thought,
maybe I shoulda handled that
right then and there.

What's he trying to do, anyway?

Could it be Chava likes Camelia?

Nah. Not worried, I can take him.

He ain't thicker than a paper clip.
He's one of those emo artist types
who knows how to style his hair
in a slick dude kinda way
and maybe he dresses with drip
like Picasso or something
all wild shapes and speckles
on his sometimes-paint-splattered pants.

I tower above the kid
and most everyone else
'cause I got Pops's gigantic giraffe legs
and my hair is never gonna
look slick 'cause my hella tight curl
loops into ringlets when it's wet

and I don't really know how to dress
outside of my hoodie and jeans.

Oh, and I got what Moms calls a "fuzzstache."
Pops tried to shave it once
but we didn't try again because
he sliced me up like Freddy Krueger
especially around my right dimple.

At the end of the day,
Chava and his wannabe artist paper clip self
ain't got nothing on me.

Plus, Camelia's *my* girlfriend now, sucka!

Play Like a Man

So here I am,
just hours into being a boyfriend
sitting at the piano at home,
the piano that belonged
to my grandpops Mingo,
who died a bunch of years ago,
trying to write a song for Camelia
and thinking it should be in the key of F
like her rainbow voice.

I hit a few keys,
play my favorite chords.
There are all kinds of wild feelings
bubbling inside stinging
like heartburn in my chest.
I want to play them through
my fingers, through my piano
but they're lodged like a loogie
somewhere in my throat.

I try again but
the music doesn't come.

My feelings flip
upside down and
suddenly the stuckness
makes me wanna give up
or throw up
and cry out of nowhere.

Pops walks in.

What's with the pedo face, Elio?

I shake my head
as if shooing off a bug.
My thick curls dangle
in front of my wet eyes.

Nada, just right here, practicing.

*Oh yeah? How come you look
like you want to cry, then?*

Pops comes over and slaps
his hand on my shoulder.
Squeezes.

You aren't being a chilletas? Right, son?

Me? A crybaby? Nah!

Well, whatever it is that's got you,
you just gotta suck it up.
That's the Solis way.

He makes a fist and
thuds it twice on his chest.

Yeah, I know.

Pops points to one of the framed pictures
sitting on the upright piano.

See my pops right there?
He never let anything
get the best of him.
He laid it all down
on the piano
or handled it with his fists.

I nod, staring at the old-time picture
of my grandpops Mingo Solis

playing piano onstage,
looking up at my grandmoms Maria,
a bolero singer.

I never noticed before
but they look like they have
their own kind of mushy pedo faces,
with, I don't know, let's just say,
   lots of feelings.

My mouth drops open
when I realize they're ultraviolet too.
But I don't say a peep to Pops.

   That was a real man, right there.
   Could have been a boxer
   but piano paid the bills.
   You look just like him,
   same dynamite face, same dimple.
   You're even playing
   the instrument he left behind
   so you have no excuse
   not to do the same.

I wanna say, I'm working on it!
I'm a boyfriend now,
and I'm trying to write a song
but it's making me wanna cry
and I don't know why!

But my tongue feels
too big for my mouth
and I trip over it.

I struggle to swallow
my frustrated feelings
thick as sick snot
trapped in my throat.

Isn't She Lovely?

Once Pops leaves,
I storm away from the piano
mad at my own dang self.

I plop down on my bed
earbuds in,
playlist blasting.
I listen and wonder . . .

If Camelia were a song
would she be a bolero
like the kind my grandmoms sang
while my grandpops played
in a smoky bar somewhere
in the 1950s in Mexico City?

Nah, she'd be a ranchera
sung till you're hoarse
from singing and crying
and burying your head in your hands.

Nah, she'd be a punk song
screaming pure fire

in a mosh pit with sweat
and spit rolling down your face.

Nah.

If Camelia were a song
she would be sugar lyrics
about magic, beauty, and being born
like the ones I'm hearing now
in Stevie Wonder's song . . .

Isn't she looovely? Isn't she wonderful?

     Camelia,
     Camelia,
     Camelia.

Yes, she is.

Mocosa Sisters

Elio, time for dinner!

Rosie snatches my earbud off
and screams into my left ear.

I shove her away
just as Tita comes tumbling in,
with her noodle-thin body
to watch round Rosie exaggerate a fall
and yelp, *Mama!*

Rosie and Tita, my two kid sisters,
are ten and eight years old but they
are like two old tías with streams of gossip
coming out of their cookie chismosa breath.

Plus, they're the grossest people I've ever met.

They started a competition in their room
to grow the biggest moco farm
on each side of the wall right by their beds
without Moms and Pops knowing.

Yup, they each dig into their noses
looking for a booger
and smear it on the wall
between their beds
where the parental units
can't see them.
They count the smears
keeping tally to see who'll
have the biggest moco farm
and be crowned the winner.

I've done a lot of disgusting
things in my life and so have my friends
but this has gotta be the sickest.

When Rosie sees that Moms
ignores her, she screams,

Mama! Elio's got a girlfriend!

Tita puckers her skinny lips at me
and makes kissy squealing noises
while Rosie keeps going,

Mamaaaa! Elio's in love!
Her name is Camelia!
I heard him say her name over and over!

I clapback,

Moms! Rosie and Tita have a MOCO far—

They dogpile me
trying to slap their hands
over my mouth
to stop me from saying any more.

Moms comes in
sees us in a tangle, pulls them off me,
lifts their chismosa chins
to look at their faces
to see if they are snotty.

Where, Elio? I don't see mocos?
Girls, are you feeling sick?

No, Mama, they say, folding
into their fake sad little eyes.

I smirk behind Moms
lifting my pointer fingers up to the ceiling
like a luchador who's just won a match.

Moms looks confused
when she dismisses us.

Vamos, kids, time to eat.
Your father has made us
yet another exquisite meal.
Go wash up.

So long as Rosie and Tita keep growing
those moco farms in their room,
I know how to keep
the mocosa sisters in check.

Dinner Debate

At the dinner table,
I am apparently the only one
who knows the art of hovering over your plate
to shovel food into your mouth
so you can finish first.

Moms says,

> *Elio! Your table manners are atrocious.*

> Rosie attacks, *Yeah, Elio. You give me asco!*

While Tita makes a gagging sound
like some dramatic echo of Rosie.

I pretend like I'm about to throw
something at them as I say,

> You're the asquerosas!

But Pops holds up his hand
and points at his mouth
asking us to play the game

of counting the hundredth
chew for each of his mouthfuls.
I'm sure it's the reason
he's got a massive jaw.

The mocosa sisters play along.
Whatever.

The annoying thing about being
the first to finish is I have to stay
for "the conversation"
and until everyone is done.

Cue: internal scream!

I have to sit there and listen
        to Moms talk about a new campaign
        she's the lead graphic designer on

        or how Rosie the nosy wants to be
        a news reporter when she grows up

        or how tiny Tita wants to be an actress
        and which princess dresses
        she hopes they'll buy her next.

Luckily, Pops is too busy chewing
otherwise, we'd hear about city planning
or the new recipe he hasn't quite conquered.

I'm telling you, it'll drive you bonkers.

Suddenly, Moms brings up
a letter that got sent home
from my school about
a social media influencer
who's doing a lot of damage.

> *Mi'jo, have you heard of this guy?* Moms asks.

I offer up all I know.

> Yeah, he's an ex-boxer
> who's got a bunch of sports cars
> and a ton of Gram followers.
> Pretty much all the kids know him.

Pops stops his chewing to listen,
moves his eyes from me to Moms,
who keeps going.

The letter says he's been having
a really bad influence on boys your age.
Causing them to treat women and girls
disrespectfully.

I shift in my squeaky seat
thinking about the dozens
of times his posts show up
on my Gram feed
even though I don't follow him.

That's not all, Moms adds.
He's been arrested for human trafficking, Elio.
He's been hurting people not just on social media.

What does that have to do with *me*?!
I say, getting defensive.

We need to know you're going to spot the danger
in men like this and not fall prey to it, Moms presses.

Rosie and Tita
are surprisingly quiet
because I don't think

they totally get it.
So I clear it up for them.

    Basically, this dude's got boys all junked out
    with too many macho beefhead ideas
    so that they don't care who they hurt.

Moms happy nods because
she knows I get it
but then, Pops finally speaks.

    Wait a minute, there's nothing wrong with being macho.
    Manning up is good for you.
    So long as you don't hurt nobody.
    Better to be a new wave macho—
    to have courage and be strong the Solis way
    than being a chilletas.
    ¿Qué no, Elio?

Moms shoots a laser mean look
at Pops but he chews away.

    No chance in hell, Pops,
    I respond quickly, hoping that'll help him
    forget how he caught me *almost* crying.

Elio, language! Moms gets all touchy.

Oops, I mean, not in a million years, Pops.

My mind runs
this way and that way
trying to understand
why Moms didn't
say anything to Pops
about being macho
and what he really means
by "manning up."

Feminists

While I clean the kitchen
for my allowance money,
Moms comes to find me.

> *You know, your pops has come a long way*
> *in challenging the patriarchy—he cooks,*
> *he cleans, he sews, all of it better than me—*
> *but there is still so much he gets wrong.*

Moms, the patriarchy?

> *Yeah, the system that gives men power*
> *over women and people of other genders.*

She pauses,
grabs me gently by the hands.

> *It's power that can become violent*
> *and toxic against anyone who challenges it.*

Yeah. I see people all over the Gram
calling their exes tóxicos when
they do dumb things to them.

Sort of like that.
But with straight men over others,
it's called toxic masculinity.

I fill the compost bin
with food scraps
and she joins in
clearing the counters.

So, does that mean
I'm automatically toxic?

No, not you, but behavior like that could be.
As a boy you have privileges that girls don't.
It's what the world gives you
just for being a boy.

I begin to scrub a dish and turn
to look at her bending eyebrows.

That doesn't seem fair. I shrug.

No, it isn't, but that's why
I'm raising you to be a feminist.
We need male allies
to help girls and women fight
for the equality we deserve.

Moms looks me up and down,
then reaches
to squeeze my cheeks
with her thin fingers
and asks,

What happened to my baby boy?

I ate him.

You sure did! Moms cracks up.

This whole feminist business
seems easy enough to do with Moms
and Camelia—ahem, my brand-new girlfriend—
I remind myself.

But with the mocosa sisters,
that's a harder thing to do
than taking out day-old compost.

Jagged Spine Kiss

One week into being in a straight solid
      RELATIONSHIP with Camelia,
Paco tells me as we walk to our lockers,

     I'm gonna do it.
     I'm gonna ask Laurette
     for a kiss.

I seriously didn't see it coming.
I suddenly realize *that's* something
boyfriends and girlfriends actually do.
     WHAT?!
It's like a lightning bolt
splitting me jagged down the spine.

Enter irrational fear number four—
     kissing.

I really like
to hold Camelia's petal-soft hand
          and drape my arm
        over her round shoulder
    easy as a waterfall

when we walk down the hall.
I mean, it makes me feel
electric.

But now Paco drops this noise
and all I can do is wonder
what it would feel like
to kiss her.
Maybe I'm too chicken
to try anything
more than
          the one-arm hug.

I'm not sure if it is
irrational to fear
kissing your girlfriend
but just the thought
makes my jaw clench
and yup, the downstairs
neighbor guy in my pants
starts to get a little happy
and I have to hide it
behind my books like
nothing's happening.

Then, just two periods later
I'm walking Camelia to class,
and out of nowhere,
      she
      kisses
      me!

She holds me
      by the face,
      smiles
      and when I smile back,
      plants
      a big fat wet one
      right on my lips.

I am pan dorado.
Toast, all crispy
      and dark on the edges
      and overdone.
I am so done.

What can I say?
I liked it!

Though I must have
a pedo face because she asks,

Elio, are you okay?

Then she tosses her head back,
opens her mouth wide as a cave,
tumbles out a laugh and sorta snorts
which makes *me* cackle
and makes irrational fear number four
BLAST OFF!

A New Way of Seeing

With that kiss,
      the radiant colors
            I started seeing since
                  Camelia came into my sight
settle on my eyeballs
and camp out.

My vision explodes whenever I'm near her.
But when I'm chillin' at home
or I'm around Moms and Pops
and the mocosas,
everything looks just like before.

Well, except when I look
at that picture in the living room
of my grands performing on a stage.
Everything in the picture
is washed over in ultraviolet
glowing the wildest neon colors ever.

Now that I think of it,
it reminds me of those
pics that capture

the true colors birds and bees see
when attracted to a flower.

I saw them when Pops forced me
to do a research paper on bees
in order to get over my irrational fear
which didn't work.

Anyway, the colors are the stuff of other planets.

I am either:
      a) being consumed by aliens, or
      b) getting wonky vision from all this love stuff and . . .

      gulp . . .

      I'm becoming like Spider-Man
      except I've been kissed by a girl
      not bit by a spider
      and maybe her kiss has given me
      the vision of a bee.

What the . . . ?

How to Walk into the Fire

Pops says,

> *The only way to get over your*
> *fear of fire is to walk right into it.*

It sounds real romantic and everything
but fearing fire is *rational.*
Who wants to get burned?

I don't think Pops
was thinking harmless things
like bees or puberty or girls
that make you scared
for no reason.

Pops gets frustrated and says,

> *C'mon, son, take a deep breath,*
> *be a buen machito,*
> *and just get over it already.*

The thing I'm learning
about irrational fears

is that you don't choose them.

There you are,
a gazelle grazing in the grass
minding your own business
and they come
to cheetah tackle you
so you feel plowed down
and bitten all over,
suddenly prey.

But I am also learning,
and maybe Pops was right,
that once Camelia liked me
and I liked her back,
I didn't feel burned
but browned like a marshmallow,
sugary and gooey
ready to be made
into a s'more.

Changes

Camelia and me sit together
swap our lunches like trading cards
but with civility and not
all robber baron style
like with the fellas.

Paco and Laurette sit with us too
which just adds to the kids
going berserk with gossip
about the new couples.

Paco says,

> *We're loverboys now.*

and I say,

> Certified. Like Drake.

But then, being ultraviolet is sorta
an inside feelings kinda thing.
I honestly can't even talk about it with Paco
though I really want to because

he's kinda a sensitive guy.
Maybe he'll think I'm weird.

I don't want to expose myself like that.
I want him to think I'm Solis strong
and not a miedoso.

I feel sorry for the loners
like Luisito, Raul, and Cheo
because I was there too
stuck in the
girls-are-too-cringy-to-even-imagine-where-I-am-now zone.
Alone.
Blue.
Wondering.

With only the boys
to talk to about video games,
lucha libre wrestlers,
and all the stuff we geek out about.

But things are different now.
Even the group chat we started
in the sixth grade for just the guys
from the school has gone wonky.

Back then, we posted nerdy cool stuff
from all over the net.
> Luisito always posted impossible jump shots,
> Cheo handled outrageous skateboard tricks,
> Paco was master of the monster trucks clips,
> Raul was the Lego and domino video guy,
> and I'd post about dangerous animals in the wild.

But as soon as eighth grade started
and the beginning of that hormone-heavy
> first week of school,
> the group chat
> has become sorta a confessional
> about who's the hottest girl
> or who has a crush
> or who got dumped.

Chava posts a different girl
he likes every day
but no one pays any attention
to him.

He says his favorite is
someone named "Amelia"
though there isn't an "Amelia"
in our school.

Could he have misspelled Camelia?
Whatever.

Luisito, Cheo, and Raul
don't post anymore and it's fine.
Maybe they have
an irrational fear of girls too.

They probably don't get why
me and Paco spend our lunches
with Camelia and Laurette.

Those girlfriend-less guys
have never been pulled
by a magnetic flower
right from the chest.

Camelia and Me

Camelia and me
are locked in and golden.
Our month anniversary
is coming up in a week.
It feels like I'm a walking
ignited Tesla machine.

We text or FaceChat ALL the time.
I tell her about geeky science stuff
I have to do for school
coding, and graphs, and my wildlife project
about the duck-billed platypus.

She sends me manga she draws,
or characters she just makes up
and they're awesome!

Writing a song for her
has been, uh, difficult.
Instead, I play
her favorites on the piano,
Frank Ocean and Kehlani.
Sabroso. Like that.

Moms and her mom even met at a PTA meeting
and approved supervised or public "playdates"
for us on the weekend
because they don't have a clue
about the smooching.
Though in all fairness
Moms has said a couple times,

It's nice you have a sweetie, but be a gentleman,

winking at me, which makes me believe
she definitely knows what's up.

Casa de Chocolates

At Casa de Chocolates
Sunday morning,
Moms drops me off right in front
while she hits the farmers market
down the block with Rosie and Tita.

I wait for Camelia,
for our "playdate,"
stare at my phone,
count the minutes before
I get to see her and be alone
in public, but still, alone.
Sweat clams up my palms
and my guts pop like rock candy.
Uy.

But when Camelia's mom stops the car
and she gets out, all glowy and beautiful,
like sunshine breaking through the fog,
I struggle to eat my cheesy grin
afraid to look too weird
while I say hello to her mom.

Sorry I'm late,
had to clean the casa
before I could come.

Don't trip, I wasn't waiting long.

Once her mom is gone,
I reach to give her
a quick bird peck kiss
but she smothers me with a long one
like cupcake smooshed on my face.

So, should we get our favorite?

Um, yeah! I'm dying for one!

A large FrozenFrío, extra canela and chile powder,
please.

I order and pay for our made-up special chocolate shake.
We drink our FrozenFrío
with the same straw, spit swapping,
which is basically like kissing in public
without actually doing it.

Exhibit A

Honestly, I've gotten used
to colors blowing up my vision
and the kissing and all that.
Grown, eighth-grade stuff.

Though we keep it to a minimum
because Mr. Trejo, my art of science teacher,
will poke his head out his classroom door
and make a big fat stink to curb it and say,

> *Gentlepeople of the jury, we have exhibit A:*
> *pubescent love!*

And everyone will holler and clap
like we're in some sorta show.

Well, everyone but that salty frito, Chava
who squints his eyes into
a skinny glare
whenever he sees
me and Camelia
together.

I don't mind Mr. Trejo because
he's a clown like Paco
but Ms. Dominguez, the dean,
she's hella judgy with kids
who kiss in the halls.

Besides,
kissing is supposed to be
the point of a relationship
no matter who is around.

Am I right?

Or nah?

Word's Out

Pops dips by my bedroom and says,

Hey, mi'jo, we gotta talk.

He sits on my bed and clears his throat.

I hear you have a girlfriend, Elio.

What? Who told you?

Moms must've told him about the "playdates."
Or maybe it was Rosie or Tita?
Almost doesn't matter who spilled the tea,
I know I've got it coming from Pops when he says,

Sí, we gotta talk, man-to-man.

Uy! Dang.

I swallow hard, hoping it doesn't have to do
with irrational fear number two: aka puberty.

Birds and the Bees

Awkward. Backward.
My heart sweats
and a funky smell pushes out
from my armpits when
Pops starts to talk.

> *Hijo, listen. There are things men got to know*
> *when their bodies change*
> *from being a little mocoso to a real man.*
> *About the birds and the bees, sabes?*

Uh-oh. He's bringing on
"the talk."

> *When I was courting your mom*
> *when we were both in college,*
> *I'd never met a finer, smarter Chicana . . .*

His face contorts like it does
after he takes a shot of tequila
and sucks on a lime all puckered and weird.
Which makes *my* ears start to feel
really hot. Like burning hot.

Pops, I say. It's okay. I know about this stuff.

You do?

Yeah. We learned it all last year
in seventh-grade sex ed class,
I say, trying to spare him
sharing TMI about Moms.

He looks like
a balloon slowly
releasing all its air.

*Okay then, good. Let me know
if you have any questions.*
He grins and pats me on the arm.

I nod and fake a smile
feeling irrational fear number two
turn my stomach into a mess of knots.

I think I'm the one who needs
to let air loose.

Seventh-Grade Sex Ed Class

It was only one class. One day.

They parted us into
a sea of two groups:
                    boys   and   girls.

The binary, how predictable.

As if there aren't more
genders on the spectrum
especially at our arts   and science school
where science is more   than science,
                    it's an art and
                    art is science.

Yeah, it was a whole pedo.
The kids protested and
come to think of it,
it was Laurette and Camelia,
before they were anyone's girlfriends,
who yelled the loudest.

We demand equal and shame-free sex ed
for all genders!
Every human comes from a menstruator
and needs to learn about periods!

And so, they let
the nonbinary and trans kids
choose their class

or both,	if they wanted
but still	kept
most of	the sea parted
in	two.

Mr. Trejo's Weird List of Sex Ed Topics for "Boys"

A whole bunch of stuff
currently scrambled in my brain
though kinda hard to forget.

> Testosterone & Estrogen
> Reproductive Organs
> Glands & Gonads
> Spongy Bodies
> Nocturnal Emissions
> Spontaneous Growth
> Egg & Sperm
> Menstruation* (only tacked on to please the
> protesters)

Basically, puberty and reproduction.

Coming from Mr. Trejo,
sex ed was a riot of laughter,
so I didn't notice my irrational fears
take too much of my miedo space.

Not on the list:

> what to do when any
> of the things from the list
> actually start to happen
> and pop off inside your body
> especially around Camelia
> and instead of laughing
> you want to fart.

Also not on the list:

> what to do when your vision
> turns ultraviolet.

Where Gonads Go

The thing about gonads
is that everyone's born
with them buried all up
in your insides.

Except that . . . girl gonads stay put
and are called ovaries.

Mr. Trejo said that guy gonads
will drop "into your potato sack"
at about nine months old
when you're just a baby.
Which made the room
howl with laughter!

But seriously,
inside the gonads are little messengers,
hormones that go and tell your brain it's time
for puberty to explode all over your body.
They make things grow, like
            your Adam's apple on your throat,
            or zits and hair on your face.
            And, ahem . . . other parts

start to bulge near the potato sack
when you least expect it,
and sometimes when you do,
but we won't go there now.

I mean, how freaky is that?

What I was too scared to ask
Mr. Trejo in a room full of smelly dudes:

Do gonads ever tell your body
to quit it with all this puberty mess?

Building Immunity

Oh! And I almost peed my pants
laughing when Mr. Trejo said,

> *It's a-okay to self-touch.*
> *It actually helps*
> *build the body's*
> *immunity.*

That's cuckoo nuts!

Who would have thought
masturbation is as healthy for you
as eating veggies?

Growing Pains

Later that night,
I get a pain in my legs so bad,
like deep-down-in-the-bone-marrow bad.

It feels like I'm getting jumped
by puberty.

Moms! I yell when
I can't take it anymore
and she comes running
stumbling through the hall
because it's the middle of the night.

My legs hurt! Aargh!

Ay, hijo. It's probably a growing pain.

She lifts
my pajama pant cuff
to the knee and rubs on
magnesium gel
and her homemade Vaporu.

Okay, give it a minute.

And almost like magic
the pain starts draining
from my legs.

Moms kisses me on the forehead,
looks at me with sweet eyes
and sighs,

> *My poor baby, you're growing so fast
> your bones can't keep up.*

> But why does it have to hurt?
> Can't I just grow fast without the torture?

Morning Rise

Moms walks in with Tita
trailing behind her, still in pajamas.

> *Wake up, corazón, time for school,*
> she says as she pulls apart the drapes
> and lets a flood of morning light
> into the room like a spotlight.

Moms stops in her tracks
when she sees me.

> *Ay!* she gasps.

I look down and my
downstairs neighbor guy
is pushing up the sheets
from underneath
like a big pitched tent.

Tita yells,

> *Don't point that thing at us!*

I fold into my blankets
wanting to cover up
and keep folding into myself
until I disappear.

Literally the worst!

Pops calls it a morning rise
the next day when he's the one
to wake me up for school.

> *We can't help it, it's a natural phenomenon.*
> *Sometimes, our guys have a mind of their own.*
> *Especially when we're knocked out.*

But Pops, why, if it's so natural,
does that bother Moms?
And why am I so embarrassed?

I wonder if she has
an irrational fear of puberty too.

> He says, *It's a private guy thing.*
> *You know, a tall puberty mountain*
> *she doesn't want to believe you've scaled already?*

What? I don't get your metaphor, Pops,
I say, scrunching my face.

Pops gives me a coscorrón.

My hombrecito's growing up
no matter what Moms has to say about it.
Right, mi'jo?

Yeah, okay, I say, smoothing over the place on my
head where he just rubbed hard with his knuckle.

What I didn't ask him was . . .

What happens if
I get a growing pain
and a morning rise
at the same time?

What will we do then?

Hey, Body

I have some questions for you.

Why you gotta go through all these
      intergalactic changes?
Why you gotta have hair
      sprouting outta my pits
      and chest and face?
Why you gotta make my skin
      pimple up
      and feel like oozing sand?
Why does my voice sound like
      gravel and glass being run over
      by a street sweeper?
Why does my heart pound like
      a punching bag being
      hit over and over
      whenever I'm with Camelia?

And don't get me started with
my down there extra bits.

Why does my neighbor guy gotta swell and chill
      outta nowhere without my doing

or thinking or dreaming a thing?
Especially around Camelia?

It feels like rockets and meteors
    shooting through the inside
    of my nighttime skies
    when I wake up
    inside a nocturnal emission—
a wet dream—all over my boxers and sheets
    and I've landed
        on another galaxy
            where I don't recognize
                the alien being
                    I am.

Yeah, can you cool your jets, dude?

I'm trying to keep it suave
and have a girlfriend over here.

Thanks,
Elio

Círculo, Mi'jo . . .

On the morning of my one-month
anniversary with Camelia,
I'm getting together the card
I wrote for her along with
some actual camellia flowers
I swiped from my neighbor's yard.

Pops sticks his head into my room.

> *For la girlfriend?*
> *Looks like things are going good.*

He approaches me
and tousles my hair.

> *Listen, son, I know our man-to-man talk*
> *was kinda messy.*
> *Back in the day, we never talked*
> *about stuff like this with our parents.*
> *Old-school Mexican beliefs, I guess.*
> *So, I told Paco's dad, Fernando,*
> *we'd join a circle he's starting for boys and dads.*

A what?

Un círculo, where we get together
with some buddies of yours and mine
and we just . . . I don't know . . .
talk about all this stuff.

You mean the birds and the bees stuff?

Yeah. And other manly man stuff.
And stuff about being indigenous Mexican.

But, Pops!

Maybe one of my buddies will be better at this than me.
Plus, there's an indio elder from Baja, California,
who's going to do some ceremonia
though I'm not sure what that will look like.

No cap, that sounds boring!

¿Qué? What do you mean, no cap?

It means no lie.

Órale. Look, I'll be learning just like you.
Besides, your mother said it would be
good for us to "explore our masculinity."

Do I *have* to?

Yeah, but first, we're hitting the cockfights this weekend,
he says, laughing and walking out.

I get the feeling
this sons' and dads' circle
ain't gonna be good.

Will we have to get
all emotional and dramatic
like Pops and his drinking buddies
when they have too much
and just listening to oldies
breaks them apart?
Will we bang on our chests
and grimace like we're lifting
something bigger than us?

I pull my breath out
of the snake den of my panza
and try not to think about puberty
otherwise I'm going to hurl
out my back end
and it won't be nice.

Oversharing Collision

As I hand Camelia her
anniversary gifts at school,
my hands shake like two rattles.

The smile she gives me
is phosphorescent
like those bodies of water
filled with tiny glow-in-the-dark creatures
I've seen on the nature channel.

She soothes my hands steady.

I get the nerve to tell Camelia
I see ultraviolet light
because of her and that
maybe it's because I . . .
I . . .
I . . . looove,
uh, I mean, liiike her.

Camelia's eyebrows lift
like two hot-air balloons.

No way! How? Which colors?

I guess she doesn't hear
the sloppy "looove-like" part.
Phew!

I close my eyes, inhale deeply
and begin,

  Ever since I met you . . .

As I speak, the hall, the lockers
swirl around me.
My heart pounds like
the thud of the bass
in a cruising lowrider.
All slick and everything.

When I open my eyes,
I can see Camelia believes me!

  I wish I could see color like that
  and put it in my drawings, she says.

  I think I might have the vision of a bee, I confess.

I pull out my phone
and show her the pictures of
the glow-in-the-dark flowers
from my research.

And you are a flower.
My flower, Camelia.

Camelia scrunches her nose at me
like she is smelling something foul.

Let's get something straight, Elio.
It's cool you see all this color
but I'm nobody's flower.

Plus, boys don't own girls, you know.

My lowrider heart crashes against
the hydrant of my spine
and I feel like a corny,
stupid junkyard car.

But it revs back up
when she lands a kiss
with her silky soft lips

right on
mine.

Then gives me
a hemp friendship bracelet
she made
just for me.

The Couples' Quad

Paco and Laurette
Camelia and me
have started our own
lunch table for couples.

We sit by the green grass of the quad
just chillin', eating, clowning.

This is when all the colors
I've seen since I met Camelia
let loose and
I feel spacious.

On the quad at our own table
where I can rest one hand
on Camelia's back
and eat my lunch
with my free hand,
where both couples can
sneak kisses between our chewing
and no one judges us
because we're basically adults,
I mean, couples, here.

We stay away from the
"make-out bleachers"
where other kids go to kiss
'cause we've got nothing to hide,
out here in the open.

Bright green grass bounces off
the dark honey of Camelia's eyes,
blazing blue birds fly around us
swooping in for worms in the mud,
and the occasional bee flies
in circular motions before
sipping on the clover flowers
that cover the lawn.

      Somehow the bees
      don't scare me here.

Cheetos vs. Takis

Our talking is playful and crowded
each trying to peck out our words
like pigeons pouncing on bread.
We aren't always kissy lovey
just so you know.

Paco: *I'm Team Cheetos!*

Laurette: *Fuchi! Cheetos suck. Takis all the way.*

Paco: *What? Takis taste like chile-coated plastic.*

Laurette: *Cheetos taste like toe jam!*

Paco: *So, you've tasted toe jam?*

Laurette: *No, tonto, I meant smells like toe jam!*

Camelia: *Wait a minute! You're both nasty!*
They have nothing but artificial junk!
The best snack in the whole world is
homemade popcorn with nutritional
yeast, Cholula salsa, and lemon. It smacks!

Paco / Laurette: *GROSS!*

Laurette: *That's hella Bay Area hippie, Cam.*

Just to get a rise out of them I say,

    No cap,
    I will eat all three *together*
    nutritional yeast,
    toe jam,
    plastic chile taste
    y todo,
    and won't even flinch!

    Paco / Laurette / Camelia: *ELIO!*

Our heads flip back.
        Laughter moves across the sky
                like a bunch of pigeons
                        taking flight.

Artwork Shine

At the bell after piano class,
I book it down the hall
to meet Camelia.
She's coming out of art class with Chava.
Her sunflower glow towering over
the booger of a dude.

He's all goofy smiley
like he's trying to rizz her up
showing her his artwork
and she comes back
with as big a smile and says,

That's tuff!

Hey! That's what she says
about my piano playing.
Ugh.

But then, Camelia sees me
      waiting
and hits me with
      her ultraviolet shine.

Gram Bam Boom

When Camelia speaks
my ears drown out all
but the melody of her voice.
Seriously.

It might be kinda mean
but sometimes I don't
even register what she says
because her words become
sweet or sharp or muted notes
dooo, reee, sooo, laaa . . .
that turn my piano brain to taffy.

But . . . today when she says
in as low a voice as hers goes,

> *Yeah, some old guy*
> *tried to trap me on the Gram,*
> *tried to trick me*
> *to be a "friend"*
> *and meet up with him*
> *when I was eleven . . .*

the record in my mind stops
with a bam scritch scratch.

But my folks caught it
before he could hurt me
and made me pull
all my pics off my page
except my art.

That's hella nuts!
I wish I could drop-kick
that guy! I almost growl.

Slow down there, cowboy,
Camelia laughs,
that was a couple years ago.
Besides, now I'm almost an orange belt
so I can kick plenty of butt.

Do you miss posting about your friends? I ask,
understanding now why she hasn't
posted anything about us.

Nah. I can share things with friends by text.
Plus, I want to be an artist so bad,

I don't mind the crackdown from my folks.
I want my art to speak for itself!

That makes sense. I nod.

The truth is, because of that scare
and other jerks at school,
I don't totally trust
dudes anymore—

I think about the group chat
and how rancid it's become.

But you're . . . different, Elio,
in a good kinda way.

Mic drop. Boom.

Mr. Trejo Soul

Mr. Trejo pulls me
into his science room
right after school.

> *Ven pa'ca, Elio. Have a seat,*
> *I want to talk to you about Camelia.*

My mind races to think about
why I might be in trouble—
    the hugging,
    the hand-holding
    the kissing.
Uy. Dang!

But Mr. Trejo is chill
like it ain't nothing.

> *What if I told you that even though*
> *I am a man of science—*
> He waves his arm across his room.
> *I believe in soul connection.*

I stare blankly because
what the heck is he talking about?

But it's scientific too, see.
What's the number one law of energy?

I scramble for the answer
and he begins it—

Energy cannot . . .

and the rest rushes out
of my A+ science class memory.

Energy cannot be created or destroyed; it can only be
shifted.

Yes, Elio, and WE are energy. ¿Qué no?

Yeah.

So, as energies, we transform and go and go.
I believe souls have companions
that make connections
over and over through time and space.

Um, Mr. Trejo, what does this
have to do with Camelia? I ask.

He laughs, adjusts
his short-brimmed hat,
points at me, and says,

Good question! I think you and Camelia
are energies that have met somewhere before.
In fact, all the people we come across
have that possibility.
Like you and me. But sometimes, we reencounter
companions who are infinite. Soul companions.
That energy is bigger and more blinding
than the rays of the sun.

So, you're saying me and Camelia are
soul companions?

Maybe. Though, keep in mind, sometimes
that companionship is shorter in this lifetime
than in others and most importantly,
here to teach us lessons.
Lessons we have to respect and honor.

Something like
popcorn pops
inside my heart
because one thing
he said I get
and it feels true.

More blinding than the rays of the sun . . .

No wonder liking
Camelia feels
so ultra wild
soul sonic cosmic.

Cockfights

Pops likes the fights—
    lucha libre,
    boxing,
    and cockfights.

Like real old-school Mexican
dirt backyard
bloody rooster fights.

Super against the law. Dang.

Pops's idea of a good time
with me is to hop on our bikes
jim jam race through the bike lanes
down International Blvd.
into deep East Oakland to Don Trino's
every-other-month prized-cock face-off.

This Saturday, we pay our fifteen bucks
to get in, which also gives us
a smackin' good carnitas plate his wife makes.

We try not to get poked
by the ginormous nopal plant
as we lock up our bikes
on the black iron fence.

The empty dirt ring in the center
is surrounded by benches
and folding chairs
filled by potbellied dudes
with vaquero hats
and plaid shirts,
pockets stuffed
with cash ready to make bets on
which of the two cocks will win.

The thing about cockfighting
is that it's really cruel
to the roosters
and mostly stupid.

They grow these pretty birds
with long tail feathers
and plump them up
so they're big and fat.
Then they make them mean.

Like they'll scratch the pickle
outta your eyes kind of mean.
Then they strap blades on their talons
and bull them to fight.

Oof, do things get gory.

Last cock left alive wins.

I've never been afraid
of the cockfights.
Not sure why,
maybe because we've been coming
to Don Trino's for as long
as I can remember
just me and my pops.

Or maybe because Pops
thinks this is what men do
and making me watch two
birds fight to the death
is his way of toughening me up.
Maybe that's why I am
not afraid of fist fighting
the way I am of other weird things.

Truth is, I don't like it at all
not like the lucha libre matches
Pops has taken me to here in East Oakland
which are all high drama and show.

I come here just so I can hang with Pops,
ride bikes together,
maybe laugh with him about
the double meaning
of the word gallo in English.

Or maybe have him ask me,
I dunno,
about music, or Camelia,
or what I'm thinking.

Or maybe I just come
for the carnitas plate.

Green Guy Aggressive

Pops gets dang near maniacal
when the fight starts.

It's like something in him
rages out from who knows where
and he goes into Hulk mode
like literally almost green,
all gnarly teeth
and muscle bulgy.

Norteño music is blasting
from Don Trino's speaker system.

Vamos, Rocky! Pops yells
at the underdog cock he's bet on.
Get him, get him!

The thing is, he ain't the only one.
All the men here
are shouting at their gallos,
taking swigs of their beers,
and looking puffier
than they actually are.

But Pops is the loudest,
the most green guy aggressive,
the most unlike himself in real life,
and it's *so* extra. Dang.

When I tug on his shirt
to ask him to sorta chill out,
he grabs me by the shoulders,
shakes me, kisses me hard
on the forehead, and laughs!

¡Eso! Isn't this the best, Elio?!

I look up at my pops
so different in this form
from the guy who runs
the kitchen at home
in an apron while humming
to his favorite Latin jazz tunes,

so different from the Pops
who reads to Rosie and Tita at night
on the couch while they snuggle up
next to him in their pajamas,

the Pops who draws a bath for Moms
when she's grumpy and "PMSing,"

the Pops who used to play
counting board games with me
because he wants me to use my brain
and snuggle next to *me*
to hear me read to him at bedtime
but then fell asleep and snored softly
while I finished the chapter
and turned off the lights.

That Pops is a universe away.

Come to think of it,
even when he isn't all
big green energy extra like he is now,
the sleepy sweet snuggly Pops
that he was with me when I was littler
is nowhere to be found.

> *We won, Elio!* Pops screams.
> *Never underestimate an underdog!*
> *Yeah!*

I don't look at the dead cock
shredded to pieces in the center of the ring
don't really care who won but
I wrap my arms around Pops
faking my happiness about the win
as if my arms can will
that old snuggly guy back,
as if my arms can bend steel.

To my surprise, the Hulky green guy
my pops has become here
slowly softens with my hug
and says like he used to,

I love you, Elio mío.

He's still in there, somewhere.

Code Word

Five weeks into being a literal boyrfriend,
Paco slips me a note during math.

Meet me at your locker at lunch.
Come alone.
Code word: Burrito!!!

The thing that worries me
about that note is the code word.
Paco and I use it only
in very extreme cases.
      "Burrito" means business.
      Cosa seria.

When I get to my locker
Paco's face is a prune as he says,

Dude, Chava likes Camelia.

Oh, yeah. Not surprised.
Plus, who can blame him?
She's only the finest girl in the whole school.

Nah, Elio, he ain't kidding.
He says he's going to take her from you
and everything.

Well, I'd like to see him try!
I say, feeling pretty confident.

Nothing,
absolutely nothing,
in the whole universe
could destroy
what Camelia and I have.

Takedown

Maybe I shoulda taken Chava down
when I had the chance.

Though I've never *technically*
been in a real live fight
I know how to wrestle because of Paco
and watching all those cockfights
and lucha libre matches with Pops.

I figure if I ever gotta duke it out with someone
all I gotta do is bust out
>a body press
>>a corner body avalanche
>>>or a bronco buster
>>or a backhand chop
>or a cactus clothesline
>>or a double ax handle
>or a big ol' butt drop
and tan tan.
It would be over.

I've for sure mastered the Blue Demon dirty look
just like my favorite lucha libre wrestler

does when he's about to demolish his opponent
'cause I've practiced that one
in the mirror a gazillion times.

The other thing about Chava is
I kinda feel sorry for the guy,
wimpy paper clip that he is.
Kicking his butt
is the last thing
I wanna do.

But I think Pops would say
I have to "man up"
so I'd take him on
with my eyes wide open.

Blue Demon Message

Next day, I let Camelia know
what Chava's been saying
and she confesses that Chava
has been texting her
a rosy red sea of sweet things!

She tells me
she doesn't want drama so
she gently turned him down.

Next time Camelia
and I are in the hall
Chava struts by,
looks our way
so I hold Camelia tighter and
bust out with my expert Blue Demon dirty look
shot straight at Chava.

Chava isn't fazed
       turns the corner
              cool, without a word.

During fifth period,
when I am up at the whiteboard
shredding a math problem,
Ms. Dominguez calls me in because Chava
reports *me* to the dean for being a menace!
Imagine, for a dirty look?
The butt brain.

Ms. Dominguez lets me go
because I never said a word to the kid
and he couldn't prove a thing
or maybe because I'm a straight-A student
who never gets in trouble.

I don't say this to Ms. Dominguez
but Chava knows
I'm sending him
a Blue Demon message
that he better not
even *think*
about Camelia
or it's cactus clothesline for him.

The Group Chat

Today, Chava has the nerve
to start a new group chat
with just me and my boys
and him.

He posts a candid picture of Camelia
sketching at the artsy-fartsy table
when she used to sit there
followed by a line of fire emojis.

Then, a string of texts
from all the guys pops up:

      Cheo: *Ooh, snap!*

      Raul: *Get wrecked, Elio.*

      Luisito: *Gotcha!*

I think of Pops, Grandpops Mingo,
and what they would do—
definitely not sit here and take it,
así no más.

No way.

My vision blurs
and I clapback
with a meme of
Jim Carrey with a bad haircut
sucking his thumb and crying
near a toilet that reads:

> *Losers gonna lose.*

And then I start to get
fire, tornado, and mic drop emojis.

Someone shoots off a meme
that declares me the winner,
a boxer with his hand raised by a ref.

Finally, I get a notice
that Chava has left the group.

Uh-huh, that's what I thought . . .
he can't handle my heat.

He shouldn't have started it.

Así No Más

But Chava wasn't done.

He started texting
nasty emojis to Camelia
like eggplants and drooling faces
and other messed-up things like,

> *I don't know why*
> *I even liked you,*
> *you aren't that smart.*

She sent me screenshots.

At the end of the day,
I puffed myself up
like a fighting cock
my fists like wicked talons
and I went looking for Chava.

Lucky for him I didn't find him.

The next day, he didn't come to school.
Paco said he heard

Chava's parents were splitting up
and he had to move or something.
Whatever.

Camelia let me jump on her phone
and I texted Chava.

>Me as Camelia: *It's Elio.*
>*I've got Camelia's phone.*
>*We're showing this to Ms. Dominguez.*

I'm not sure if it was my threat,
his parents' divorce, or what
but Camelia said
he stopped texting her.

Así no más.

Laundry Land

My room looks like a monster
ingested a twelve-ton truckload
of clothes and threw up all over it.

It's a landscape, my masterpiece!
I tell Moms on Saturday—laundry day.

Ay, Elio. Have a little self-pride.
You're growing up.
You've got a sweetie and a fuzzstache
and you can't clean your own room?
Don't even get me started on showers!

Elio's room smells like it got skunked!
Rosie says, pushing the door open
to my room while holding her freckled nose.

Get out, chismosa!

I throw a dirty sock at Rosie
and it bounces off the mass of curls
covering her forehead.

Elio! Moms shouts. *Watch yourself with your sister!*

Tita, right behind her, says,

> *Yeah . . .* her big eyes looking around,
> *it smells a puro pedo!*

Then makes a fart noise
with her little pouty mouth.

> Maybe my room does smell like farts
> but at least I'm not growing a double moco farm.

Moms looks confused but
shakes it away and says,

> *Look, you want to live in filth in here, fine.*
> *But out there, you will clean up after yourself.*
> *I'm not anyone's cleaning service.*
> *Not yours, not your sisters', not your pops's.*
> *You got me?*

> *Yeah, not your cleaning service,* Rosie smirks
> as Moms turns to go
> and they walk behind her.

I toss a pair of my sweaty boxers at them
hoping it'll catch one of the mocosas
but it doesn't.

The two sound like screeching hyenas
as they book it out the door.

Rosie yells,

> *¡Puerco! Dirty rotten pig!*

And I fall onto my bed
laughing.

Brick Load

I am building a ridiculous
online world on *Mindcrack*, while I wait
for a load of laundry to be done.
Pops yells from his room
and I yell back from mine,

> *Elio! We're going on a bike ride.*

> Is there a cockfight today?

> *Nope. We're going to find out about this circle.*

> Aw, Pops, do we *have* to?

He comes in and shoves a pile
of clothes to the side.

> *Yes. It's over at the community garden*
> *where Paco's family keeps a plot.*
> *It'll be good to get your head out of that phone—*
> *get some fresh air.*
> *Build those lanky legs so that*
> *they're thick Aztec legs like mine.*

Pops winks and raises his shorts
to show his muscles.

But Paco told me they have a beehive!

So what?

Pops! C'mon, gimme a break.
You know how I feel about bees.

Gotta walk into the fire, son.
You gotta practice confronting your fears
if you're going to get over them.

Just when I thought
Pops had forgotten all about
the dads' and sons' circle,
he lays all this on me
así no más.

Great.

Fernando's Community Garden

Pops and I bike to the community garden
not too far from where we go to watch
the cocks fight.

We swivel through crowded traffic,
the thud of deep bass
pounding out of tricked-out cars
with too-big rims on the tires,
cruising by bunches of trash
from a houseless encampment
that looks like art to me but isn't,
a hairy man in a suit spitting some sort of gospel
in Spanish from a megaphone
in front of a check-cashing spot
that's next to a taqueria selling pupusas
and Oaxacan-style mole tamales,
and señoras with fruit stands on ice
selling big cups of mango sandia mix for seven bucks
while their kids play in a shopping cart.

It's our East Oakland bike groove
and though it might not be pretty to others,
with Pops,

it's the color and sound
of home to me.

When we arrive, Fernando, Paco's dad,
gets up from tending some plants
and shoots off a loud whistle for Paco to come.

The place is huge!
It's an abandoned lot
a bunch of folks just took over
right here off International Blvd.

Paco's been telling me about this place.
Their house doesn't have much of a yard,
and Fernando is crazy about gardening,
so he uses this space to do his thing
and he makes Paco work here on the weekends.

Paco never told me
        how big and cool it was
        how much food they grow in twenty plots
        and how the beehive is safely hidden
        behind some bushes.
        They planted a bunch of fruit trees
        in barrels in a circle

to shield the noise of cars and fumes
and their forest green color
bounces across the lot
with golden washes
in the Saturday-morning sun
in this urban jungle.

Paco never told me
how much I'd like it either.

Temazcal

Fernando and Paco
take me and Pops to a clearing
where there is a firepit
and a brown dirt hut.

Fernando calls it a "temazcal"
a sweat lodge like our relatives
in Mexico use for cleansing.

The one here is built outta mud and rocks
and the pit is filled with volcanic stones
which they brought from Mexico
and the whole nine.

Fernando says our group of guys
which he's named "Brothers Rising"
is going to be learning about
puberty, consent, and our spirits
but first, we're going *into* the temazcal
to do a ceremony when the elder comes
next weekend.

We're gonna start by building a fire in the pit
to get the stones piping hot.
Then we're gonna strip
      down
        to our
        chones
and go inside
the temazcal.
Almost naked!

Then the elder is gonna guide us
in song and prayers
and then they're gonna
      put the stones
        into the center
        of the hut
        with us in it!

Then they'll pour water
on the hot rocks
so the steam
      spits   into
      the   air
and oozes into our lungs
and makes us

s
w
e
a
t.
Like a freakin' sauna. Uy!

Fernando says we're gonna have to take it
like the men we are becoming
to get rid of old bad habits
and let go of fears.

Maybe this is Pops's way of making
me literally
        walk
                into
                        the
                                fire.

Dang!
Being as naked as a toad
around other people
in what's basically an oven
has given me a NEW irrational fear.
It totally bulldozes
how much I like this place.

Consent-O-Rama

As we walk through the garden,
Fernando says,

>Becoming a man will take more than a sweat.
>It's learning to balance our emotions,
>our desires, and our urges, especially
>with our romantic partners.

Pops and Fernando for sure have talked
about Paco and me being coupled up
with Laurette and Camelia.
Ugh.
I can feel a puberty talk coming.

Fernando asks Paco and me
if we've ever heard of consent.

>Yeah, it's permission, Paco says.

Pops bows his head quietly,
looks hella uncomfortable.

I honestly don't mind this talk so much
coming from Fernando since he's a

community organizer for teen boys in East Oakland.

> *Yeah, mi'jos, it's as simple as that.*
> *Do you have permission to look at, talk to,*
> *touch, be near, or spend time with that person?*
> *If the answer is no,*
> *even if there is a slight hesitation,*
> *then you don't have consent.*
> *You feel me?*

Fernando pulls a weed
from the ground and
whispers,

> *Con su permiso.*

I must look like a
lost tourist because he explains
that when pulling anything
from Mother Earth, we also ask permission.

I think about Camelia
and all the times I've never asked her
if I can hug her or even give her a kiss.
But then I think about the first time
she gave me that jagged spine kiss

and only asked if I was okay
after she'd smacked it on me.

So I ask,

> But what if you're in a relationship?
> Like you're a boyfriend and all that.
> Don't you have built-in permission?

Fernando nods.

> *It would stand to reason that yes, you do,*
> *but the truth is, real consent is when*
> *you get permission even when you are in a*
> *relationship.*
> *It's what girls and all people deserve,*
> *even you, no matter what.*

Being a boyfriend gets more
complicated by the day but
being with my ultraviolet Camelia
is all the way worth
getting it right.

Maybe being in Brothers Rising
won't be so bad after all.

When I'm Grown

I lie in my bed at night,
my phone turned in,
arms behind my head,
mind spinning into the still darkness.

I'm trippin' over what Fernando told us
about consent and how tricky
becoming a man can be.

The picture of my grands in the living room
floats into my thoughts.

      The two of them playing music together,
      the notes like colorful sparrows
      swirling around them
      and how suddenly after Camelia,
      the image became wild with color.

Were their souls connected too
like Mr. Trejo said?

I wonder what I'll be when I'm grown.
           A piano player like my grandpops?

Definitely not a singer like my grandmoms.
Not with this crackly voice.
I've got the grades to be a city planner like Pops.
Or a graphic designer like Moms.
Maybe something to do with animals?

Moms says she doesn't care
what I choose
so long as I'm doing what I love
and I'm a gentle and caring man.

In all honesty, I can't think that far ahead.

I sometimes miss my old self
        my little-kid, pre-beesting self with
        no irrational fears crawling around,
        no body morphing,
        no heart thudding.

Right now, though, there's so much
to like about growing up.
        Ultraviolet reds, oranges,
        yellows, greens, blues,
        indigos, violets

swarming my blood
in a warm bath of light.

I want to always have that
because it means
> my feelings for Camelia
> will still be swirling
> > like sparrows
> > > from my heart.

Duck-Billed Platy-Creep

While doing research for my project
on the duck-billed platypus,
I gotta read about mating.
Human reproduction is weird enough
but in animals, mating is literally WILD.

The male platypus basically hounds
the female platypus for weeks
chasing her in the water
until she is ready to mate.
He even bites her tail!

That's just rancid.
No consent for miles.

Who would want to be
with anyone who hurts them?

Isn't love supposed to be
soulmate sunshine and roses
and ultraviolet streaks of colors
spilling all over,
like it is for me?

Mating Rituals

Mr. Trejo says
mating is necessary
in order for life to be.
Animals and humans
all come from this process.
Sorta fascinating
and sorta gross.

I'm still freaked out about
how aggressive the male platypus
gets when trying to mate.
He reminds me of Chava
trying to get with Camelia.

I never want to be that rank
when it's my turn.

Wait! Is this my turn
to do mating rituals?
Maybe not fully? Right?

Maybe I can get away
with stopping this speedboat

pushing through the waters of my body
making all the zigzag feelings
crash inside me.

Thinking of mating rituals
makes me slightly nervous,
but it doesn't quite qualify as
an irrational fear yet
since I don't seem to want to fart.

So I take four deep breaths,
and remember I'm still a kid!

I scratch my head
and with it
      push
            my wild ideas
                and worries away.

Friday with the Fellas

Camelia is absent
from school today.
The halls of our school
feel hollow.

Laurette says Camelia is sick.
I don't text her.
I figure I'll do it after lunch.

I avoid our couples' table,
leave it all to Paco and Laurette.
Without Camelia
I'd be a squeaky third wheel.

Instead, I find the fellas,
spend lunch with
Cheo, Raul, and Luisito
like old times,
tell them about
the duck-billed platy-creep
being a dirtbag y cosas así.

Luisito shoves
his phone in my face
and yells,

You've got to see what Cheo and Raul made!

They spring on me
a video panning across
an entire mock underwater city
of Talokan built entirely
with Legos and some cardboard!

Ooh, snap! From *Wakanda Forever*, that's fire!
I say and body pile on top of them.

Lunchtime goes by
lightning quick.

Having fun with the fellas on a Friday
I forget to text Camelia
before the bell rings
and I have to get to class.

Puberty Stuffs

When I get home,
I FaceChat with Camelia
como nada.

The vein on her forehead
        is bulging.

Uh-oh, she's mad.

        You didn't even check on me during lunch, Elio!

        I didn't want to bother you.
        I figured you were home and needed rest, I lie.

I feel a lump of remorse
tangle up my throat for forgetting.

        Aren't you even gonna ask what's wrong with me?

My top lip starts sweating
and my stomach is now
popping weirdly.

Oh. Sorry. Yeah. What happened?
Are you okay? You don't sound sick?

*Do I really have to walk you through
being a boyfriend, Elio?*

I see her hand lift
and smack down on her bed.

She gets quiet suddenly.

*I got cramps, like really, really bad cramps.
I couldn't walk.*

Where, like a charley horse on your leg
or something? A growing pain?
I get those. They're the worst.

No, Elio! My period cramps.

Oooowh!

My face flushes magenta
my saliva feels like grass
as I swallow.

Gulp.

She's *actually* talking to me
about periods.

PERIODS.

Like blood from the uterus
and all that menstruating
period stuffs.

Then my mind flashes to Mr. Trejo's
goofy sex ed class
and how some of the guys
called it "Aunt Flow" and "La Comadre"
and I sorta crack a smile.

> *There's nothing funny about it!*
> Camelia starts to cry. *It hurts a lot.*

I feel like a buttwad
but I can't find the words
to say anything other than
a measly,

That sucks.

It's like my tongue
is stuck on a frozen
glass I just licked.

Look, I gotta go, she says.

And the
FaceChat
goes
click.

My Heart Song

My heart beats
so loud,
I hear it
in my ears.

Throbbing.

I close my eyes
and search
for the music
inside it.

I want it to come out,
to express my rhythm

ultraviolet
but scared

like Grandpops Mingo
except he wasn't scared.

I want to have
his flower hands,

to play a song
I write for love.

But every chord I hit
sounds dissonant.

It's not grooving
to the rhythm inside.

So I give up
and just record
myself playing
Post Malone's
"Sunflower" love song.

I send it to Camelia
and she listens to the audio text
but she doesn't even
respond to say
she got it.

Dang.

Alive and Kicking

Talk of her puberty stuffs
is honestly way scarier to me
than my own puberty.

Proof that
my irrational fear
of all things pubescent
is not all the way gone
but alive and kicking.

In my head,
I hear Pops say,
Walk into the fire.
Maybe I shouldn't have been
such a booger about it.

Lemme hop online real quick,
to see what the deal is
about period cramps.

. . .

Ooooh!

The net says period cramps
are muscle contractions
sorta like poop cramps!

Your body's muscles
are pushing something out—
a uterus is pushing out
an unfertilized egg
and your guts, a big old deuce.

Sometimes it hurts
and sometimes it doesn't.
One article said that junk food
can make it worse.

Though the uterus does it monthly
and your guts are supposed to do it daily.

Whoa! That'd be a double whammy
if you got period cramps and poop cramps
at the same time.
¿Qué no?

Oof.

Note to self: Kick back on the junk food.

Feel-Better Bag

I hit up Moms.

Will your homemade Vaporu
help more than growing pains?

Why, where does it hurt, mïjo?

Uh, uh, well, uh, I mean, for cramps.

Yes, of course, my herbal rub is strong medicine.
It'll help any achy pain. Show me where?

No, no, it's not for me. Um, uh, it's for Camelia.

Camelia?

Yeah, for her, uh, period, um, uh, cramps.

Ah! Pobrecita. Here, why don't we put together
a feel-better bag for her?

A what?

Moms hands me a cloth bag from her drawer
and a new glass container of her Vaporu
and says,

> *What else would make you feel better*
> *if you weren't feeling well?*

I imagine Camelia
curled up in bed
and think about
how much it sucks to be sick,
to have a growing pain
twist you up inside.

> I dunno, something warm?

> *Okay, like what?*

> Socks, maybe a beanie?

> *That's great! Now, qué más?*

All of a sudden,
we are moving around the house
filling the bag with

a pair of fuzzy socks,
a small hot-water bottle,
some red raspberry leaf tea—
        Moms says it's good for uterus cramping—
and some dark chocolate—
        Moms says our ancestors called it cacao
        and it's medicinal too.

Camelia's puberty doesn't seem
so scary anymore
though I don't know if
this feel-better bag
will make her un-mad.

Whoosh Boom

On Monday,
Camelia is back.

She feels far away,
like a-long-road-trip distant.

When I ask her why
she says,

> *I don't expect you to understand, you don't bleed.*
> *But a little sympathy would have been nice.*

> I'm sorry, Camelia, falls out of me
> like broken teeth.

I stand there
holding the feel-better bag
unsure how to give it to her
so I make a seriously goofy face
and open my arms
like a blanket.

She snorts, covers her mouth,
and comes in for a hug.

When she puts her head
on my skinny chest, she says,

> *Elio, I can hear your heart.*
> *It makes a whoosh, whoosh, whoosh sound.*
> *Isn't it supposed to sound like boom, boom, boom?*

She looks up at me and smiles
all her Camelia radiance on me.

> I dunno? I must be special like that!

I raise my eyebrows
up and down quickly
like a clown
to make her snort
and make us all better
again.

Brothers Rise

Forget what I said about
Brothers Rising being
not so bad.

When we all strip down
to our boxer shorts
an irrational fear
starts to inch its way
          up my spine
                    into my head
          and back down
to my gut.

Don Manuel, the elder
in the ceremony, removes
their skirt and pants
but keeps on a cotton loincloth
and the beads around their neck and wrists.

Their face is brown, with deep lines
          spraying out into their temples
                    when they smile.

Fernando says,

Welcome, young brothers, to this special day.
We are entrusting your journey, this rite of passage,
your rising from adolescence into manhood
to Don Manuel Cázares, a Xochihuah,
a nonbinary Nahua priest from Baja, California.

Just at that moment,
I squeeze my glutes together
like trying to tighten a valve,
but an irrational fear-propelled fart
s q u e a k s   out   of   my   butt.
Uy.

Paco gets a whiff and starts to giggle,
his upper torso bouncing up and down
without a sound, his chubby cheeks jiggling,
his sand-brown skin reddening.

And like dominoes,
        I start laughing
        and then our friends catch on—
        Raul, Cheo, and Luisito—

and they start stifling giggles
until Raul bursts out, *Pedo!*

Then our dads start laughing
because the fart hits their noses too
and then Don Manuel gets a whiff
and we're all rolling laughing

high on my fart
like skunks drunk
on their own stench.

Energies of the Body

The only way we recover
from those giggles is when
Don Manuel's robust voice
falls on us like armor.

Young sons, the energies of the body
manifest in many ways.
Yes, in laughter like babbling brooks,
in sadness like winter clouds
or in terror or pain or love . . .
so many ways to let the power
of our creator, Ometeotl, flow through us.
All are true because
they come from the universe.
In this journey, we will be learning
how to harness their power
for the benefit of ourselves,
of our family, of our community.

Camelia drifts into my mind
and it intensifies
my color senses.
I see the elder's skin

turn translucent as they speak,
around them, a soft light
emanating golden orange.

They continue,

> *You are dawning into new ways.*
> *You will learn to hold*
> *your feminine and masculine energies*
> *inside the same soul.*
> *This is the way of the young warrior,*
> *for a new path of peace needed by the world.*
> *We must disconnect from*
> *the ways of the colonizers*
> *who taught us to hate ourselves.*
> *In hating ourselves, we have learned to hate*
> *our duality and divinity and the world—*
> *our women, children, elders, our Xochihuah,*
> *our most wounded.*

The golden light around Don Manuel
shatters and comes together
as if it is throbbing and moving
to the rhythm of each of their words.

We cannot be burdened by the conquest any longer;
it is time to rewrite our present
and revive our connection to all living beings.

I look at Paco—a cosa seria expression
splattered across his face
and I know something big
is about to happen
when we go into
that sweat lodge.

I swallow hard
as this thought
comes over me.

We will go in boys
but might actually,
for reals,
come out
men.

I don't think I'm ready.

Inside the Temazcal

As we step into the sweat lodge,
I hold my hands over my crotch
hoping somehow that will
make me feel less exposed.

The elder's prayers fill my ears.

> *We are in the womb of Tonantzin*
> *to be cleansed.*
> *Mother Earth will help us*
> *let go of all that is burdening us—*
> *all of our toxins, gone.*
> *In her body, this oven,*
> *we are born anew.*

The steam storms its way
into the air and mixes with the
hot breath of all of us in here—
Paco and me,
our dads,
Raul, Cheo, and Luisito,
and their dads.

Don Manuel's prayers
grow strong,
echoing in the hut.

Oh great spirit, Ometeotl
whose voice sings in the wind,
whose breath gives life to the world,
hear us.
We need your strength and wisdom.
May we walk in beauty . . .

The heat makes my head
feel light. Camelia swirls
ultraviolet in my mind.
My eyes cross.
Camelia is smiling.
Her soul is smiling.
The burning air pushes against my chest.
I feel like I might pass out like I did
when I was little
and got stung by a bee.

Make our hands treasure your creations.
Make us wise so that we learn things
you have taught your other children,

lessons you have written
in mountains and streams . . .

I must look like a mess
because Pops hands me a wet towel
and tells me to cover my face
and just that little bit of cover
helps me stay awake.

Make us strong, not to be superior
to our brothers and sisters but able
to fight our greatest enemy—ourselves.
Make us ever ready to come to you
with clear eyes so when life fades
as the setting sun,
our spirit may come without shame.
Tlazocamati, all my relations.

The songs pound through
my eyes into my temples
and down my neck
into my heart.

I'm too woozy to be scared.
Whoosh, whoosh, whoosh.
Camelia. Camelia. Camelia.

Beating.

Mr. Trejo's voice saying,
Soul connection.

I lean my head on Pops.
My mind is coming in and out.

I hear again . . .

> *We are in the womb of Tonantzin to be cleansed.*
> *Mother Earth will help us*
> *let go of all that is burdening us—*
> *all of our toxins, gone.*
> *In her body, this oven,*
> *we are born anew.*

A New Warrior

Paco backhand slaps my bare panza
making me exaggerate my stumble
out of the lodge.

What the heck was that?

I'm too thirsty to answer,
my mouth baby powder dry.

All of the guys shake off their
sweat like wet dogs as they exit.

Is this it? Paco asks. *Is this what it means
to be a new warrior?*

I shrug my shoulders
my brain feels wobbly and light
but I say,

Nah. We're supposed to be men, except I feel
like a man who's gonna throw up, fool.

Imagine.

Paco's eyes stare
right through me
up to Oakland's
darkening sky.

We are now men, Elio. Real men.

I look up too,
see the violet-blue cloud shadows
circling above,
my heart remembering
its steady beating,
and I throw up
a little in my mouth.

Wuss Out

So, what'd you think, son? Pops asks.

I'm not sure
I want to give my true answer—that it sucked.
I don't understand how sweating like a dog
will make me a man, but all I say is,

I'm feeling crazy dizzy, Pops.

Here, hydrate, it'll help, and he hands me a water
bottle.

Pops slaps his rough hand
over my hand and taps it.

*This sure as heck
isn't the way I came up
all spiritual y todo.*

*Your grandpops Mingo
put boxing gloves on me
and shoved me in the ring
when I was younger than you are now*

and if I ever cried,
he threatened to hit me harder
than the hit that made me cry
in the first place—the Solis way.
But I think it was a good lesson.
We can't wuss out when things get rough.
I'm proud of you today, son.
Your grandpops would be too.

In this sweaty mess
my breath returns
and fills me with pride too.

I didn't wuss out.

I feel closer to Pops
in a new way that
isn't around watching fights
and maybe, just maybe
I am closer to actually being
a man.

With Who?

When I get home
all I want to do
is call Camelia,
feel her sunlit sweet smile
soothe me.

I FaceChat her but she doesn't answer.
Though she texts,

> *@ Casa de Chocolates*
> *getting a FrozenFrío*
> *call u later?*

With who? I ask.

While I wait to hear
who she's getting our favorite
frozen chocolate smoothie with,
    I crash on my bed
    feeling heavy
    and burnt from
    the inside out.

Corpse Silence

Pops wakes me up
the next morning for school.

My body feels all sore and stiff.
I must have slept like a corpse.

I go get my phone from
its nighttime spot in the kitchen.

I check it.

Camelia didn't call or text.
Nada. Just left me on read.

No matter, I can't wait
to see her today at school.

Maybe she'll see
a difference in me?

Chava Returns

At school, I see Chava
before I see Camelia.
The dude's back and acts
like nothing's happened.
Like I don't exist.

Good. Let's keep it that way.

But then, Paco hands me
another "Code word: Burrito" note.

> *Chava is calling you out.*
> *To box. After school.*

I hesitate. Don Manuel pops into my head.

> *Let go of all that is burdening us.*

Nah, that's different, I figure.
I ain't gonna wuss out.
I'm gonna *walk into the fire*
like Grandpops and Pops.

I'm gonna have to
            take
            Chava
            down
            once and for all.

Chava is literally
a head shorter than me
so I know it'll be over with quickly.

But we never make it to the fight.

Ms. Dominguez gets word of it
and she brings us both in
to have a restorative circle
which is just fancy speak
for trying to make us squash it
in front of adults.

At the circle, Chava's chest
            is all puffed out
                        like he's a big balloon
            or something.

Oh yeah, I think,
let me just pull out my phone

and show Ms. Dominguez
the kind of sucio this weasel
really is.

Before I can do that
Chava has *his* phone out
                    and is showing Ms. Dominguez
                    and *me* the love texts
                    between him and Camelia!

I can't believe what I am seeing.
My girlfriend,
        the strongest, prettiest flower
actually likes this guy!

Apparently, she said
there is something "forbidden"
about Chava and that
she understands him because
they're both artists, plus
her folks split up too
and she likes "the thrill of him."

I mean, YUCK!

I want to scream
and pound his face in
with a double cactus kick.
I feel like my insides   are melting.

My ultraviolet
        sight
            glitches
                    like a
            broken   computer   screen

the light   so   frag-   mented

I have to close my eyes
for the rest of the meeting.
            I say nothing
            as Chava's smug voice
            and Ms. Dominguez's voice
                            fade like the end
                                of a song
                            I never want
                            to hear again.

More Than a Bee

I want to look for Camelia
to see if it's really true.
What would I say?

It hurts.

More than a growing pain,
more than a stomachache
or holding an imploding fart,
more than a beesting.

I walk out of that room,
feel the sadness claw into me
like a cat's scratch.
I swallow my hurt into my chest
and it lands somewhere in my heart.

When I get home from school,
all I know to do
with this mess of feelings
is bury my head in my pillow

and cry
as quietly as hovering bees
looking for honeysuckle
in clover-less grass.

So quietly Pops won't hear
and question the man
I am supposed to be now.

Lovesick

Elio, mi'jo, are you all right?

Moms places a soft hand
on my crying head
buried in my pillow and plays
with the wave of a rogue curl.

I go cold because
I'm supposed to be a solid man,
a warrior, and all that.

I lift my face, puddled by tears
to see a frown crowning her eyes.

¿Qué te pasa, Elio? Tell me. Is it Camelia?

How does she know?
But I say no anyways.

Moms squints her eyes
like she doesn't believe me.

I have no place to put all this hurt
so I only nod and suddenly
tell her everything, in surrender.

The more I talk, the more
it hurts, and the more I sob.

I'm sorry I'm being a chilletas.
I can't help it, I say, wiping my eyes
with the back of my hand.

No, mi'jo! You know with me it is always okay to cry.
There is no better medicine when you are lovesick.

Lovesick?

Yes, mi'jo. Love is what makes us human but also,
what can break our hearts open.

That explains why it feels
like I am being split right here.

I touch my chest. Moms
puts her hand over mine.

It will take time to get over. Give yourself the space.

But how, Moms? How?

*Self-love and time will find a way to heal the seams
and you'll be stronger than you were before.*

My puddles of tears
grow to an ocean of sadness
where I feel I might
drown.

Tender Rosie

Once Moms is gone
nosy Rosie pokes
her curly-haired head in my room
and doesn't say anything
for a change.

But she must have heard everything.

She sits right next to me
though I turn away from her.

She digs a few fingers
into my curls and scratches
my scalp lightly and sings
the melody to a lullaby
"Duérmete Mi Niño"
that Moms used
to sing to us
except Rosie
can really sing in tune
'cause she probably
got the singing gene
from Grandmoms.

I hear my sister's tender
voice in the key of G
and wonder if she'll
ever have the nerve
to break someone's
heart like Camelia
so I turn to her with
my crushed crying face
and say,

Don't ever be a cheater, Rosie. Okay?

She just nods
and keeps on singing.

Tapping Tita

Tita comes in
and sits down
next to Rosie.

Two stink bugs
turned butterflies.

She taps my back softly.

Her hands feel like
soothing drops of rain, falling
when she says,

Crying is okay. Is okay, Elio. For everyone.

Before Her Light

Before Camelia's light
    my world was
    something else.

I didn't know what
love was but
I also didn't know
a breakup
would feel like
    quicksand,
    dynamite,
    anime drama left and right,
    a call that won't connect,
    a bike rack turned on its side,
    a missing tire,
    getting shorted one
    chicken wing in your order.

Before her light
    my heart didn't ache
    I didn't see ultraviolet
    all the time.

Now that she is gone
    and I can't hold her hand
    or play her favorite song
    much less write her one
everything is wrong.

Wet Vac Clapback

Later, when Pops gets home,
I hear Moms stop him
from coming in my room.

I zoom to sit up and
suck up every last tear
like a wet vac.
I hear them whisper.

Why's he crying?

Camelia. Let him be.

Aw, come on, honey.
He can't let her get the best of him.
He's a Solis, there are more fish in the sea!
After that sweat, he's supposed to rise to manhood
not get all wussy over some chiquilla.

Quit with the beefhead talk, viejo.
Elio is tenderhearted. You know this about him.
Didn't you say that sweat helped YOU understand
your feelings as a man? Let him have his.

Could you both just PLEASE leave me alone!
I yell, from behind the door,
unsure where my own angry voice came from.

I hear Pops stomp off to bang
pots and pans in the kitchen
and Moms walk lightly
to the living room.

I dive back
into my trance
of lovesick sadness
trying to breathe.

The Winner Chat

Chava hops on
the boys' group chat
and brags . . .

> *I bagged Camelia.*
> *Who's the loser now, Elio?*

And adds
the same Jim Carrey meme
I sent him.

Wildfire Red

Something fiery flickers
inside my ribs and
I want to smash Chava's face.

I want Camelia to hurt too.

Suddenly I am seeing
angry, wild red.

Camelia cheated on me,
broke my trust.

Now I want her
to feel my fire.

Rotten Things

A list of rotten things I wish
for Chava *and* Camelia:

They get stung by a thousand bees.
They stink like eight-day no-shower smelly boxer shorts.
They face-plant into a patch of poison oak.
They always step on dog dung when they walk.
They scrape their elbows bare whenever they fall.
They get a case of uncontrollable farts.
They grow a face-full of whiteheads.
They almost choke on a tortilla chip.
They get suspended by Ms. Dominguez for kissing.
They get brain freeze when they eat a FrozenFrío.
They have a visible case of nonstop boogers in their noses.
They develop incurable giant dandruff.
Their armpits smell even with deodorant.
Every dog growls, every cat hisses, every baby cries when they
get near.
A whole flock of pigeons poop on their food when they eat
lunch outdoors.

I wish they never see ultraviolet.

Can't Shake It

Everything appears
in washes of red.
I can't shake it
from my eyes.

At school,
      I slip,
            slide,
                    and maneuver
through the halls
so I don't run into them.

I stay away
from the couples' quad
where Paco and Laurette
now hang out,
alone.

I'm doing pretty good
until
I see Camelia's
unmistakable streak
of blue hair

shining inside
all the red
as I line up
for laps
on the track
during my PE class.

It's the first time
I've seen Camelia
since her burn.

A pain
pinches
inside
me.

Make Out

Camelia doesn't walk freely.
  Chava pulls her toward
  the make-out bleachers.

Blood rushes through my veins,
my face swells with heat.

Just as the coach whistles
  and the class
    takes off running,
the blue streak in her hair
turns a deep red.

I pause.

Stare, shoot lasers
  right at them.
  Only Camelia sees me.

    She hesitates.

  But Chava tugs on her hand
and she starts walking again.

She turns to face me
curls her fingers up and down
into the tiniest wave
when he isn't looking.

Was it meant for me?

Volcanic Dark

The hypocrite!
The liar!
The cheat!

Anger whooshes
through me,
a coraje so red
I detach from my body
and start running.

I run faster than
I have ever run.
I'll show her what she's missing.
I'm way better, way stronger
than that paper clip,
I mutter under my breath.

I catch up to the class
and pass them,
tears and anger
splashing across my face
but I don't care.

My chest moves up
and down as if my heart
is going to push out
        of my ribs
        straight through
        my skin.

Each breath feels
like I'm burning inside
and the dirt track
starts
        to swerve
            as if it's
        melting
beneath my kicks.

Suddenly, I feel a shock
                a pain right in the center of my heart
                    which doubles me over.

My
world
drains
of
color.

The ground is gone,
    I am falling
        falling
                into an endless dark pit
                    about to be singed
                    on piping-hot
                    volcanic stones
                    miles inside
                    the earth's core
                    where the darkness
                    snuffs out
                    my breath.

Tearing

There was a time when the dark scared me.
Not long ago, I'd see big eyes and snarly teeth
suspended in the obsidian air.

This isn't that kind of thing.
This is more of an emptiness.
Where there is
>   no movement
>   no sound
>   no air
>   no heartbeat.

I am pulled out of it by the touch
>   of a hand on mine.
It feels warm and urgent.
Asking me to come,
calling me without
calling my name.

So I open my eyes and see
Moms's crying face crushed in fear.

Mi'jo. Elio. Despierta, amor.

Her hand squeezing my hand
like mush.

When I really focus
I realize I am in a doctor's office
or a hospital room?
Pops is speaking
with someone in a white coat.

How can he have an undetected heart condition?

*It is rare but sometimes strenuous exercise
can cause a small hole in the heart to tear.*

A hole, in my heart?
Is that what she said?
It's all so fuzzy.
I feel like I did the time
I had an extra baby tooth removed
and they gave me blue pass-out liquid to drink.

This will be a robotic, minimally invasive surgery.
It has risks, but we do seven hundred procedures

a year here at Children's Hospital Cardiology.
He will be in very capable hands.

I am not sure what it means
because I feel brick heavy.
Pain comes from something
sticking out
of the fold in my arm—
the area around my heart
feels bruised and achy.

All I want to do
is close my eyes again.

Broken

In the fog, the memory of passing out comes to me.
    The watery ground.
        Not finding my footing.
  Camelia and Chava.
  The bleachers.
      Paco holding my head
        before I was lost
        in the emptiness.

Moms shakes me a little.

    Mi'jo, do you know your name?

But all I can think about is
        Camelia.

Was she hesitant with Chava?
I saw it right before I fell out cold.
Something isn't right
but I don't know,
I could have been hallucinating,
it could have been wishful thinking.

The doctor speaks up again
and this time, her voice is not
jumbled but clean as a blade.

He'll have to stay home until the surgery.
No school. No sports. No agitations.

That seems harsh.
Why can't he just go to school? Pops says.

He needs to stay calm so as to keep from fainting
again.

Dang. I get it all of a sudden.

Camelia broke my heart.

Like literally right in two.

Grandpops's Inheritance

Híjole.

Turns out I inherited
more than piano genes
from Grandpops Mingo.

Pops said he died young
of an enlarged heart
they couldn't do anything
about back then.

Moms says maybe
his heart was so filled
with love for Grandmoms Maria,
it just kept growing
until it burst.

Pops says, nah.
It was just bad genetics.
Love ain't supposed
to kill you like that.

Who knows,
maybe Grandpops Mingo
and me are soul twins.

Our hearts are all stuffed with love
and both of ours broke
just for different reasons.

Miserable Maybes

Maybe it wasn't Camelia
and my heart broke by itself.

Maybe it was the irrational fears
that started the day the bee stung me.

Maybe I was sorta showing off
by running too fast like some raging macho head.

But maybe it *was* because she chose
a creep like Chava over me.

Maybe I didn't really know
how to be a good boyfriend.

Maybe she was never
as good as I imagined.

And maybe, just maybe
she and Chava deserve to be miserable together.

Maybe it's best I stay away from them
until my heart gets better.

Group Chat Challenge

The group chat blows up with messages . . .

Luisito: *Hey bro, hope you're okay. That ish was scary!*

Paco: *Yeah bro, the ambulance taking you away all knocked out was the worst!*

Me: I'm okay, just surprised I'm that sick. I literally had no clue. I low-key thought it was just heartburn or something.

Raul: *Yeah, get better, bro. When's the surgery?*

Me: A month. Doc says I got to get strong again.

Cheo: *Lucky you don't have to come to school tho.*

Me: Still have to do work packets or I'll lose my As.

Paco: *Bro, that could have happened to you in the sweat lodge.*

Me: No doubt. I almost passed out there too.

Then suddenly, Chava chimes in.
I'd forgotten he was even on.

> Chava: *Broke your little payaso heart, eh? (Laugh emoji)*

> Paco: *Buzz off Chava, no one wants you here.*

> Chava: *Yes they do 'cause I have a challenge. Anyone who shares a pic of a girl showing the most skin wins.*

> Raul: *Bet.*

> Cheo: *Bet.*

> Luisito: *Bet.*

> Paco: *idk*

> Chava: *I'll start.*

He sends a pic of a
Sports Illustrated supermodel
in a bikini.

Raul: *That's easy! You can get almost anyone*
from the net!

Chava: *True. Then the double-down challenge is,*
send a pic of a girl you know. I've got a juicy
one of Camelia on deck. Elio might appreci-
ate it.

Me: Nah, I'm out. Makes me sicker to play
into your stupid little creepy games, Chava.
Grow the hell up!

I leave the group chat thinking
a jerk like Camelia
deserves a jerk like Chava.

But then I text Paco
and ask him to stick around
to be my spy.

Double-Headed Lucha Libre Quarantine

My bedroom is
where I wait to get strong
for my surgery,
where I've started drawing my favorite
lucha libre fighters, wrestling,

where I imagine I am Blue Demon
and Chava is Moco Face going toe-to-toe
and I pound him like a pancake
with one double hacksaw smash.

Hey, I gotta have some excitement.

Moms works from home
on her computer all day
so she pops in and out of my room.
Not even knocking.

I know she's worried and also
making sure I'm not on my phone
"mindlessly scrolling."

Moms catches me drawing
a girl with a blue streak in her hair
wearing a skintight lucha libre suit
with big bouncy boobs, horns,
and a dog's tail.

> *Elio . . .* She nearly scowls at me.
> *Remember what I said about toxic masculinity?*

I got nothing.

> *This is it. Right here.*
> *And don't you tell me that isn't Camelia.*

I don't know what to say.

It's like I'm a two-headed dragon
with one head for my feelings
and the other for my mind
and they speak two different languages.

> *Mi'jo, you have to do better.*
> *Love is going to hurt when it's gone*
> *but hating on Camelia is not the way to fix it.*
> *Maybe talking about it with your dad*

or with Fernando or
Don Manuel will be helpful.

I wince a little when she says that.

Or cry, mi'jo.
Crying and just letting yourself
be honestly sad about it
will help it move through you.
I promise that would serve you
and others so much more.

I'm sorry, Moms.

She goes to take the drawing
from my notebook but
I tear it out, crumple it up,
and throw it across the room.

Gram Ultraviolet

When Moms leaves,
I hop on Gram
    and scroll
    and scroll.

I find Camelia's page.
    I know.
    I can't help it.

I go through all of her posts
    one
    by
    one.

Mostly, Camelia's got process posts
with the back of her hand
drawing and painting
all these super normal things
and making them really beautiful
    like vines and plants,
    a messy room,
    or people at a bus stop.

Mixed in are clips of
    her and Laurette's hands
    making Mexican hot chocolate
    or of her pet pug sleeping
    or of her trying on
    the fuzzy socks I gave her.

The only post of actual people
is a video of us hanging out
at the couples' quad
    piggyback races
    with Laurette and Paco
    all of us
        tumbling
            on the grass,
                laughing.

Suddenly Camelia posts something new!
What timing!

It's a time-lapse
of her drawing
a real live heart,
with valves and veins,
all anatomically correct and everything.

But then,
she draws barbed wire
 across the heart
 and pierces it
 with one of the spokes.
 She draws a pool of blood
 at the base.

This has got to be
her grisliest drawing ever!

All the caption reads is,
"Corazón herido."

A wounded heart?

Paco on My Side?

Paco calls me days later and says,

Chava was just bluffing, the dude sent nada.
I think he was trying to rub it in your face.

That booger gets me so mad
I could punch something.

Relax, Elio. Don't even think about them.

Yeah, you're right. *She* chose the jerk.
Trash deserves trash.

I wouldn't go that far, Elio. Camelia is still cool,
still Laurette's bestie, though she did do you dirty.

Paco! Whose side are you on, anyway?
She literally broke my heart.
I wouldn't be in this mess if it weren't
for her backstabbing, lying,
straight mentirosa head!

Kick back, tóxico.
Look, just stay away from them,
and you'll be good.
All right, bro?

All right, but promise you'll let me know
if Chava sends out Camelia's pic.
If nothing else, I should see it too.

Bro, honestly, I might tap out.
That challenge doesn't feel right.
Remember what my dad said about consent?

Yeah, so what?

I'm just saying, I think sharing pics
of girls we know goes against that.

Let Camelia suffer, let the pictures roll!

You ain't right, bro.
Those heart meds they've got you on
must have made you stone-cold.

I've got a broken heart, Paco.
So what if Camelia gets one too.

Chava Baboso Face

Out of nowhere
I get a text from Chava
the slime face.

She's mine now pendejo,
he texts.

Then he sends
three pictures of Camelia
in her bikini
lying out in the sun by the beach.

She's showing more of her skin
than I've ever seen.
More than a normal bikini
is supposed to cover.

He ends it with,

For your eyes only,
and a laugh cry emoji.

I respond with a poop emoji, así no más.

Burning Comet

I stare at the pictures
and instead of feeling victory
because I've seen them,
I'm all twisted up with, I dunno,
      sadness,
      jealousy,
      attraction,
      guilt
because now I have them.

A collision of feelings
blisters me
like molten lava.

I try to lie still
but a red cloak
takes over me.
Blood rushes
to my chest
and I hold myself
above my heart
feeling like

I'm turning into
a burning comet.

If LOVE sent me
to the stratosphere,
HATE shoots me
farther
out
into
the
universe!

The Biggest Burn

The biggest burn
would be to share
Camelia's pictures
on the group chat
before Chava does
to make her hurt
more than me.

Talking Mess Text

Camelia: *I hear you're talking mess, Elio.*

Me: WTH? No I wasn't. Why are you texting me? Don't you have a boyfriend to text?

Camelia: *Laurette told me that Paco told her that you said I'm trash! How could you?*

Me: How could *YOU*?

Camelia: *What?*

Me: You didn't even have the nerve to tell me to my face that you liked Chava and we were done. Not even thru a text.

Camelia: *I didn't want to hurt you, Elio. You're a really nice guy and I'd like to be your friend again. That's why it hurts to know you were saying things about me.*

Me: Well, check this out, I also told Paco that you are a backstabbing, lying, straight mentirosa head. Did he tell you that?

Camelia: *Elio, this isn't you.*

Me: Yes, it is. It's what you made me.

Camelia: *I didn't make you anything, you are choosing to be a jerk.*

Me: I'm the jerk? I'm not the one who cheated. I'm also not the one who sent bikini beach pics to Chava.

Camelia: *What?*

Me: Yeah. I know all about them.

Camelia: *Did you see them?*

Me: Probably the whole boys' group chat did too. Real classy, Camelia. Real classy.

Camelia: *OMG! I can't believe he did that to me.*

Me: Doesn't feel good to be betrayed does it?

Camelia: *That's not fair, Elio. This really sucks.*

Me: Like I said, you are trash and you deserve all the trash you'll get with Chava.

Then, I block her.

More Broken

I turn over on my bed.
My body drops
into the mattress
like a big rock
into a valley of sadness,
shattering.

I don't think I've
ever been so mean
in my whole life.

And my heart has
never felt more broken.

Living Piano

I drag myself to the piano
and I hit the keys
so hard the pictures
on it shake.

Moms comes running in
pointing at her phone
and mouthing,
I'm on a call!
before turning to go
into her bedroom office.

I slouch over the piano—
my arms and head slam the keys
when a framed picture falls and smacks
me on the shoulder before
landing on the piano bench.

My grands' soul connection
radiates from the picture.

I know the song
I imagine they are playing—

about a love so true,
they carry
their love's essence
inside.

"Sabor a Mí" . . .

Every time I play it,
Pops always says
it was their favorite.

But I'll never have
a love like theirs.

Picture Love

Just then, Moms walks in
no longer on the phone.
She looks lovingly at the picture
of the grands I'm holding
and she says,

> *Everyone said your grandparents' love story*
> *was the greatest ever.*
> *You can almost hear the music they made*
> *by the way they are looking at each other,*
> *qué no?*

I nod slowly because I do see it.

> *Y mira, your tío Esteban's love story*
> *with your tío Gilberto is also pretty awesome.*

Moms picks up my tíos' wedding
picture and smiles at it
like they can see her.

> *Though sometimes it takes a few times*
> *before you find the one,*

like your tía Lucy who had two husbands
before your tía Helen came
and swept her off her feet.

I start to see colors
fill each of the pictures.

You know what makes many couples' love special,
Elio?

I shrug.

They bring out the best in each other.
Just like your dad and me do.
Sure, we don't always agree but that's okay,
we are all works in progress, always growing.

I think about how Moms
stopped him from
scolding me for crying.
How she has to school him sometimes
and is patient when he gets it wrong
because she loves him
new wave macho flaws and all.

Will you play something soothing, mi'jo?
Play your abuelos' favorite song?

Moms rubs my back briskly
as if to say, get going.

I put my grands' picture
back on the piano
and place my fingers on the keys.

As I inhale, fluorescent colors
burst from all the people
in the pics who have really loved.
They swirl around me until
I hear the sound of bees,
birds chirping,
and my own heartbeat.

Their love takes hold
of my breathing
and settles like mist
quietly inside me.

For the first time,
I am not afraid.

Snitch Fever

After a week and a half of resting,
my parents think going
to a Brothers Rising meeting
will be a mellow enough
answer to my cabin fever
especially if we only talk
and stay out of the temazcal.

I don't entirely want to 'cause
Paco the snitch is gonna be there
but I go anyway.
I can't stand one more second
of being alone.

Fernando fist-bumps me
but when Paco says,

    Hey, bro,

and continues to prepare the fire,
Pops and Fernando look at us like
they are trying to guess the drama.
But then, Cheo, Luisito, and Raul,

and their dads walk up and distract them.

I am so pissed at Paco.
He's a dirty rotten backstabber
just like Camelia.

I got to be better about hiding it.

The Man Circle

Without Don Manuel here,
Fernando leads us in an opening
prayer while smudging himself
with a stick of palo santo
and passing it along.

Ometeotl, great spirit who blesses all things,
we give thanks to you and to the Ohlone people,
original caretakers of this land.
We ask permission to hold space for all
that is to come from our spirits today.
May our young ones be strengthened
as you have strengthened us,
to choose a righteous path
that loves and respects all beings
for the healing of humanity
living on Mother Earth, Tonantzin.
Tlazocamati, Ometeotl.

Young brothers, before we begin . . .
Fernando turns to us.
Let us agree to be guided by this wisdom.

En lak ech—you are my other me.
If I do harm to you, I do harm to myself.
If I disrespect you, I disrespect myself.
If I am good to you, I am good to myself.
If I honor you, I honor myself.
Now, he says, *I have one question for you . . .*
What is weighing on your shoulders?

We all sorta fidget and shift in our seats,
a whole bunch of knuckleheads
not knowing where to start.

Let It Out

Paco's eyes start to water
his face turns into a series of wrinkles.
He drops his round head as he admits
he's nervous about me being sick
and how scared he was
when he saw me pass out.

Paco's crying stirs
something in me.
His crying reminds me
Paco is my other me.

So I go over
        sit next to him,
        tap his back,
        and give him a one-arm
        it'll-all-be-okay hug
and then I cry a little
along with him
before I admit I am
scared of the surgery too.

Don't worry, sons, go ahead and let it out.
We got you, Fernando says.
Keeping things bottled up
can really harm all of our relationships
and can affect our mental health.
We are breaking cycles of harm here.
Let it out. We got you.

I surprise myself by not caring
that Pops is watching.
When I glance over,
he nods and rocks himself,
with eyes closed.

I can't even imagine
what's bouncing around
Pops's head
as the tears drop down
        my face.

Puber-tea

Raul and Cheo got more puberty
tea going than I realize.
Stuff we couldn't talk about
in Mr. Trejo's class
or the group chat
or in person.

Cheo wants to know how much
is too much self-touch time.
Raul's having feelings for
boys, girls, and nonbinary people.

Here in the circle, talking about puberty
feels easy, like something I needed
but didn't want to admit.
I guess now I wanna know the answers
more than I am scared of them.

The council of dads whips around
advice that actually makes sense:

> *Self-touch time is perfectly normal.*
> *Most everyone does it*

but it's gotta be done in private.
You just gotta find a balance
and not let that be all you do
and you gotta not hog the bathroom.

The answers to Raul's question
come in with the same kinda swing:

> *It's normal to like more than one gender.*
> *Sexuality and gender are two different things*
> *and both are on a spectrum like a rainbow.*
> *Most importantly, don't stress*
> *because you love who you love and that's okay.*
> *Plus, you've got lots of time to figure it out.*

Then the dads talk about
how they worry about kids
on their phones, what they call
"the one-eyed brain-sucking monster"
and how social media influencers
are hijacking our brains . . .

I sorta go quiet and notice how Pops
is the only dad who doesn't say much.

Whatever it is clanking around
his head must be really loud,
maybe too much to say?

Then my mind spirals,
        my color scheme skews
                into Camelia's ultraviolet smile
        but that image
                        crashes against
                the reddish fire
                of another crushing image,
        Camelia and Chava
        up in a tree . . . K I S S I N G.

The two of them acting as toxic
as that influencer dude on social media.
Rank. Just rank.

        Elio? Pops says,

staring me down
to put me on the spot,
expecting me to spill my tea.

If I do, will he?

More Fish in the Sea

My voice quivers and cracks
when I begin.

> I *almost* got into a fight
> with this guy over a girl, I say.
> I mean, she cheated on me
> with him and I wasn't going
> to let him get away with it.
> I really liked her but
> she chose him over me.
> The thing is, I don't
> think she's *that* into him.
> He's a real bonehead.
> I'd like to kick his butt
> just to shut them both up.
> Whatever,
> she's just stupid,
> a stupid girl,
> and not even worth it.

I notice Pops again,
his eyebrows lift
in two hairy arches.

He pushes his lips up to a smile,
nods, he looks so proud
it's like I can hear his thoughts
clearly now:

> *That's a Solis. That's my mijo.*
> *There are more fish in the sea.*

But he doesn't say it
and none of this feels right.

So I stop short of saying anything
about the group chat challenge
and the pictures Chava sent me.

It stays a brewing fire
in my guts.

Got Your Back

Fernando stares into the flames
and speaks slowly at first . . .

> *We've come into this circle*
> *to learn from one another*
> *as growing, flawed men,*
> *and so I hope you hear my words . . .*
> *In all our actions,*
> *we strive to honor ourselves*
> *but also to make space to honor*
> *the women and girls we love*
> *and care for in our lives,*
> *past and present.*
> *En lak ech.*

Pops listens,
puts his palms together
in front of his mouth
like he's waiting to
say something too
but Fernando goes on,

It's important to never let your ego
stand in the way of treating her respectfully.
Calling her stupid and worthless
because you're mad 'cause she might have
treated you unfairly does a lot of harm.
It disrespects her but also tarnishes your word.
It moves you away from integrity and kindness.
In other words, just because someone hurts you
doesn't mean you have to hurt them back.

I squirm in my chair feeling
something start to crumble inside me.

Now Cheo's dad, Albert,
speaks up.

Women and girls got it hard.
Life is set up against them,
to make things easy for us
not for them.

Luisito's dad, Roy, says,

Yeah, and that's why
we have to be their backup,

we have to be there for them.
We have to work for things to be fair.

I look at Pops
hoping he'll have my back
but he only stares at the fire.

Dry Ice Pops

Wait a minute, Pops! I say,
acid like anger bursting from me.
Are you really backing them up?

Elio, cool it. Your heart, he says firmly,
coupled with a wreck of dagger eyebrows
like he's embarrassed or something.

Aren't you gonna say *anything*?
You're the one who tells me stories about
Grandpops Mingo and how he handled everything
with his fists and now all of a sudden
fighting is bad?

Pops doesn't even flinch
he's colder than dry ice.
He shakes his head a little
and bites down so his
jaw muscles puff out.

No, son, you misunderstand.

My talons come out of nowhere
and I scream,

Pops! How can you be such a hypocrite?
You tell me not to cry or be a wuss.
You take me to cockfights!
And I don't even like them!

Pops stands
and I think he's
gonna rip into me
in front of everyone
but he clenches his fists
and walks away.

Raul's dad follows
and tries to pull him back
to the circle.

Fernando turns to me
and puts his hands
around my cheeks
and I try to pull away
but he holds me gently.

I can see Pops watching
from a distance.

Fernando centers
his eyes on mine.

> *Elio, being brave, being a good man*
> *is letting things go sometimes,*
> *letting go of hate, letting it flow,*
> *whether it is in our tears, or in our sweat,*
> *letting it go expands us,*
> *in the same way river water*
> *runs into the ocean.*

I breathe in and out,
out and in with Fernando
and slowly,
a calmness
settles on me.

I inhale.

I exhale.

I am beginning
to understand.

The Right Thing

When I get home,
I open up Chava's text
and delete
all Camelia's pictures.

If these pictures go out,
they ain't coming
from me.

The Moms Ambush

Moms swoops into my room
in an angry ambush.

Elio, do you have inappropriate pictures of Camelia?

What? Uh. No, no. I don't.

Give me your phone.

Moms, I don't. I swear.

*Luisito's mom just told me that someone's passing
around pictures of Camelia in her bikini.
You better not be doing that!*

For reals?

Moms doesn't answer
but unlocks my phone
and scrolls through my texts.

What's this group chat?

Moms reads the entire exchange
about the double-down challenge.

Who is this Chava boy?
Is this the guy who is with Camelia?

She shoots off questions
like rounds of fire.

I feel my ears turn hot
and my heart thuds.

I see you tapped out of the challenge.
I'm proud of you for that, mi'jo.

She scrolls.

Wait, y esto? Elio? What!

She's reading Chava's text
the one without the pics
I just deleted.

For your eyes only?
What did he send you, Elio? Eh?

Nothing.

Mi'jo, this is abusive toxic behavior.
For your good and for Camelia's,
you better not have kept anything, Elio.

You won't find a thing.
Keep checking, I don't care!

I raise my voice so loud,
Moms stops and looks up
from my phone.

Elio, nobody here yells at you
and you will not be the one to start.
Plus, tu corazón,
you've got to watch your excitement,
she says more calmly, and takes a deep breath.

Okay, okay. I'm sorry!

I rub my face with my hands
to stop from crying.

Then she says,

But you called her all of these names?
Mi'jo, I'm surprised at you.
How would you feel if someone
said these things to me or to your sisters?

I'm sorry, Moms, I repeat slowly.

Thank you, but I'm not the one
who needs your apology most.
You have to find a way
to make things right with Camelia.
Until you do, I am keeping this phone.

But Moms! I scream. That isn't fair!

She turns to me and
gives me a look
more powerful than words.

In it, I understand:

She doesn't deserve toxicity
and neither does Camelia.

Moms walks out of the room
speaking to herself.

Poor Camelia, I've got to call her mom.

I lie in the ditch
of Moms's ambush
without my phone
to sew up my wounds.

Fusing

Head back.
I close my lids.
Tears trapped
behind my eyes.
Breathe.
Feel.
Hear the soft
hum of bees
somewhere in the distance
fusing into the notes
of "Sabor a Mí."

Ultraviolet colors
crash and disappear into black,
back and forth
until I am so dizzy
in a world of color
and colorlessness
I can only sleep.

Medicine Dream

I am in a temazcal with
Pops, Paco, Fernando,
we're in our boxers
sweating buckets.

Don Manuel chants
except it isn't them
it's Grandpops
with his flower hands
playing
that are my flower hands
our hearts beating
at the same tempo
bees coming to the
notes I play
not stinging
but feeding.

His voice is
medicine that
covers me in a
steam of healing.
I sweat.

I tear.
I flow
          love like foaming river water
                         expanding into
                                    a moonlit ocean.

I am sorry.
I am so sorry.

When I wake,
I know what
I have to do.

Surveillance

When I tell Moms I need my phone
to call Camelia to apologize,
she reluctantly gives it back.

She seems suspicious and stands there
with her arms crossed like a prison guard.

Can I have some privacy, please? I ask.

*Okay, but know that I will find out if you don't make
amends.*

I hear the floorboards creaking
just outside my bedroom.

Moms! I can hear you!

I wait for Moms's footsteps
to walk away, and then
I press FaceChat.

FaceChat Forehead

My heart pounds
like a thousand drums.

Camelia answers but only
shows me her forehead
and a hint of the blue streak of hair.

> *What do you want?*

> I want to say I'm sorry.

> *Whatever, Elio.*
> *Leave me alone.*

She hangs up.

I call back.

I get her forehead again.

> Can you please hear me out?

> *What?*

You were right. I was a jerk to have said
all those nasty things about you.

Camelia lowers the camera
so I can see her eyebrows
and the tip-tops of her eyelashes.

You really hurt me when you cheated
but I should have said that instead of
trying to get back at you.
I didn't know what to do with all my feelings
and I wanted you to hurt just as much as I did.

Her eyebrows crowd
like crinkled paper
as she lowers
the camera and I see
her honey-hazel eyes
watering.

I owe you an apology too, Elio, she says finally.
*I'm sorry I cheated and so sorry for the way you
found out.*

Why *did* you cheat on me, anyway?

I thought you didn't care because
you didn't call me that one time I got sick
but you did give me the feel-better bag
which I loved so much. I was confused.
You were actually good to me,
you didn't deserve that.

Do you mean it?

Yeah. I really do.

Thanks. I needed to hear that.

I really don't know why I was even
attracted to Chava.
Yeah, he's also an artist but he's been
mean to me since the beginning.

You know, he sent me pictures of you
at the beach but I deleted them.
I honestly wanted to send those pictures out.
That's how mad I was at you.
But something stopped me.
Remember those ultraviolet colors I saw
when I was with you?

Well, that's the color of love for me.
And if I want to have it in my life,
I got to do right by people,
especially those I love.

You love me, Elio?

Yeah. I'm not afraid to say it. As a friend.
Are you okay with that?

At last, Camelia shows me
her full face, nodding,
tears running
down her round cheeks.

Elio, can I tell you a secret?

I nod as I wipe
my teary eyes.

Chava's been forcing me to kiss him
when I don't want to.

What? You aren't giving consent?

No.

Aw man! I thought I noticed something funky
when I saw you going to the make-out bleachers.

Yeah. When I try to push him away,
he gets really pissed off.

That's so messed up! You have a right
to give your permission
for every touch even if you are
boyfriend and girlfriend.
He should be respecting you.

I know, doofus. You don't have to mansplain.

Uh. Sorry. I didn't mean to speak for you.

I have to break it off with him,
but I'm sorta scared of him.
If you got nasty with me when we broke up,
I think he will be worse.

You might be right about that, Camelia.
Us dudes can behave like tóxicos.

But you don't have to be
a duck-billed platypus.

A what?

I mean, you shouldn't be with someone
who isn't good to you.

I know. You're mansplaining again.

Sorry. I wish there was something I could do.

You're doing fine. Listening is enough.
I've missed having someone as nice as you to talk to.

Camelia and I talk
for another hour,
face-to-face friends
like nothing bad
ever happened
between us.

I tell her I thought
she broke my heart
but it was really genetics

and about the minimally invasive
robotic surgery I'm having
that's going to repair it.

It
      feels
          so
              good
                  to be
                     healing.

Chancla Stomping

I call Paco to tell him
Chava's been hurting Camelia
and he's gotta be stopped.

> I need to be the one
> to defend Camelia.

> *Kick back, macho man*, Paco says.

> No seriously, I tell him,
> I'm bigger than Chava.
> I can snuff him out
> in one round.

> *You can't do it now, bro,*
> *remember your heart condition.*

> I don't even care
> what happens to me
> that chancla has
> gotta be stomped.

Chismoso

I know my bro by now.
He's a chismoso
but I still love him.

He's probably gonna tell Laurette
who's for sure gonna tell Camelia.

That's okay by me.

I want Camelia to feel good—
I want her to know
that without her having to ask
something's going to be done
about Chava.

I Text Chava

Me: Chava, you better leave Camelia alone.

Chava: *Jealous much, pimple wad?*

Me: I ain't jealous. You just need to keep your
        stinky paws off her.

Chava: *She's mine. I leave her alone when I want to.*

Me: You can't own anyone, you butt brain.
        But tell you what, I'll fight you to settle it.

Chava: *Oh yeah. You and your army of pendejos?*

Me: One-on-one. Meet after school tomorrow at
        the park across from school. I win, you leave
        her alone. You win, I leave you both alone.

Chava: *Haha! Bet. I ain't worried. I'm going to have
        fun crushing your weak little pissy heart.*

I leave him on read.
We'll see about that.

Missed FaceChat

I don't pick up Camelia's
FaceChat.

But a long audio message
comes through my text.

She says she isn't some
damsel in distress who needs
saving from a man.
She can handle it herself.

She says I better not
fight him or else
she's never speaking
to me again.

If I have to lose
her friendship,
it will have been worth
stopping that idiot
from hurting her
anymore.

Early-Bird Butt Whoop

The next day
I tell Moms I'm going on a walk
just to get out of the house.

I put in my earbuds
and head for the park.
I gotta be on time
to kick this jerk's butt
right into the ground.

I review luchador moves in my head.
    Body press
    corner body avalanche
    bronco buster
    backhand chop
    cactus clothesline
    double ax handle
    big ol' butt drop.

Psych myself up by playing
the *Karate Kid* song,
"You're the Best."

The wind blows in my face.
It's all good.

I get there before the bell,
sit on a bench, and see
that baboso head Chava
staring back at me from a classroom.

Then suddenly,
he appears at the school doors.
He must have asked
to be let out early.

All right, all right.
Early-bird butt whoop.
I don't blame him
for not wanting to be humiliated
in front of the whole school.

Square Up

Just as Chava crosses the street
the bell rings and kids start
streaming out of the school
flying behind Chava
like a swarm of bees
on the loose.

I steel myself.
My vision swirls red.
My heart is steady.

Chava comes up.
I stare him down
and say,

      Square up, baboso.

Chava throws
the first punch
and hits me in the neck.
A surge of fire shoots
through my veins.

Camelia screams,

Elio, don't!

Paco comes behind me.

C'mon, bro, cut it out.

I push his grip off
my shoulder.

Seeing I'm distracted
Chava tries a sucker punch
but I step back
and he just misses.

I clench my fist round as a boulder
and deck him square in the mouth,
knocking him to the ground.

Luisito, Cheo, and Raul
are yelling,

Bro, bro, stop, bro!

As I'm about to move on him
like Blue Demon with a bronco buster,
I see my pops and Fernando
and the rest of the dads from the circle
and Mr. Trejo like blurs of light
running toward us.

Paco must have told them too.
Good.
I want them to see me
do right by Camelia.

The swarm of bees
roars in my ears
but I am not afraid.

See me, Pops,
      in a cockfight,
      an enormous gallo,
      blades out
      going in for
      the kill.

Be proud, Pops.
      En lak ech.

Like you.
Like Grandpops Mingo.

I bend over Chava
to pin him to the grass

        but Chava   kicks me

          in the soft center
           of my chest.

          I stumble back
      feeling split   by pain
          down the middle

          a rainbow of color
   fragments into   a   million pieces

      then   starts to   fade

      until suddenly
everything goes

           dark.

Through Time

I am in space
floating
through galaxies.

Fernando pumps my chest
Pops blows air into my mouth

I am a comet
burning through atmospheres.

Fernando counts, one, two, three as he pumps
and Pops blows deep long breaths into my lungs.

My blood sings
to the movement
of stars.

Pops is so scared, he's crying.
He's crying!
Fernando shouts, *Keep going! I'm feeling a pulse.*

I am a filter
of light inside

and outside
of time.

      Soul shifting.

                    That's it. We're getting him back!

I breathe.

                        We've got him back!

I am
red,
orange,
golden,
green,
blue,
indigo,
violet,
an ultraviolet boy
who has loved
and is alive
in the universe.

Winner?

When things come into focus
I'm in the back seat of Pops's car,
Mr. Trejo riding shotgun,
my head is on Camelia's lap.

Did I win? I ask her.

She's a wreck of tears
though what seems like relief
tumbles out when she hears me.

Nobody won, doofus. Nobody.

She flicks me on the arm.

Where are we going?

Pops turns over his shoulder
his face crushed
and wet with worry,
and anxiously says,

We're taking you to the hospital, son.
Just relax.

I'm sorry, Pops. Are you all right?

It'll be okay, mi'jo, try to rest.

I look up at Camelia and say,

I just didn't want him
to hurt you anymore.

Camelia whispers
so Pops
and Mr. Trejo
don't hear her.

That was so stupid, Elio!
If you wanted to be an ally,
THAT was not it.
My god, I hate that I even have to tell you this!

I nod, unable to speak.
I made such a macho mess
of everything.

I tell Mr. Trejo,

> I know what it's like
> to be galactic.

He reaches out
with a fist bump
I weakly match with mine.

I'm secretly glad we're
going to the hospital
'cause I don't know
how much more my heart
can take.

The ER

Moms and my sisters
arrive at the hospital
just as I'm put on a gurney
and moved through the ER.

Moms grabs my hand
and kisses me on the head.

I'm here, mijo. We got this, okay, she says breathlessly.

Gracias, Moms, I say as she walks on the other side
of the gurney from Pops.

Moms reaches across me and
wipes away the tears tumbling
down Pops's face.

I suddenly realize their love,
the feminist and the new wave macho love
that brought me to this world,
is a hella messy work in progress.
But it steadies me
as I goof up

and feel myself grow,
take some good from each of them
and learn to be myself.

I turn back to the ER
waiting room and see
      Camelia taking my sisters' hands
      joining Laurette, Paco,
      Fernando, and Mr. Trejo
      in the corner of the room.

I feel good my sisters
will be kept safe.

I wish I could say the same
for myself.

The Loser

Minutes melt into hours
before they let me go
with strict orders
not to exert myself
until the surgery
in a couple weeks.

Everyone I love
is still in the waiting room.

Rosie and Tita warm me
with hugs.

Tita starts crying.

> *I thought you were gonna die*, she wails.

> *No way, not this knucklehead*, says Rosie,
> misty-eyed.

She buries her head again
into my arm and hugs tighter.

Thank you all for being here.
Thank you for saving my life,
Pops, Fernando, Mr. Trejo.
I'm sorry I put you all
    through that.

They crowd around
taking turns to hug me,
a total loser,
but really loved.

Fernando says,

> *C'mon, Laurette, Camelia, Mr. Trejo,*
> *Paco and me will take*
> *you home.*

This loser is
more grateful
than ever.

Car Cry

Reclining, riding shotgun
in the car on the way home
alone with Pops I say,

Pops, are you disappointed
I didn't really man up?

I think I'm the one who failed you, son.
I'm so sorry.

How?

By not teaching you earlier
what to do with big feelings.
I thought being a new wave macho
was all courage and strength
on the outside.
I didn't realize how being a man,
a true new wave macho,
is about courage and strength
on the inside.

Pops taps my chest over my heart gently.

> *Being a chilletas, losing,*
> *running, winning, loving.*
> *Todo eso makes us human, mi'jo.*
> *It scared me to know you hurt,*
> *so I encouraged you not to feel*
> *like I stop myself from feeling*
> *when emotions are strong.*
> *It's hard to walk into the fire.*

A trickle of tears
falls lightly against his
massive jaw.

> *But we have right now to learn.*
> *I'm still learning how to become a good man.*
> *Loving your mother, and fathering you*
> *and your sisters, Brothers Rising.*
> *It's all making me rethink what I was taught.*
> *And you, you are teaching me that*
> *the Solis way includes el corazón.*

I listen and watch
as Pops stops the car.

His face opens up,
it welcomes a river of tears.

The Pops from when
I was little is here again,
a Hulk-less watery,
vulnerable, beautiful mess.
He reaches
to hold me.

Together we swim
in the letting go.

Check Myself

I hear my sisters
playing moco farm
in their bedroom
as the morning light pours
through the drapes.

I think about what a challenge
they could have if they run into
a don't-know-what-to-do-with-feelings
dude like me.

I gotta do better.
I gotta check myself
and not let anyone have
to do it for me.

Check myself
when I do things
to hurt girls
even if I don't mean to.

Check myself when I hurt
other guys too.

I cringe just thinking
of all the possible ways
I could have acted
to help Camelia
instead of boxing with Chava.
And how I also called Chava
all those nasty names
and busted his lip.

I gotta . . . scratch that.
I *will* do better.

Open Heart

Good morning, mi'jo.

Moms walks in
to give me a cup
of hot cacao.

How are you feeling this morning?

I'm feeling.

*That's a great thing. For anyone. How 'bout your
body?*

I'm a little achy but mostly just weak.

*I am so grateful your pops and Fernando
were there to do CPR.
With your condition, we could have lost you, mi'jo.*

I nod with a half smile
hoping to stop her moist eyes from flowing
and hoping she will forgive me
for being such a macho head.

I love you, Elio. You've always been my sensitive boy.
Don't let growing up into "a man" rob you
of being able to show your hurt in ways
that will heal you and not hurt others.

I take a sip of the hot cacao
and I feel a soft warmth
grow in my chest.

I love you too, Moms.
And thanks for being patient with me,
even though I've been a pain in the you know what.
I really get how I gotta do better by you and all girls,
even Rosie and Tita.

Moms wraps both her
hands over mine as I hold
the cup of cacao she's given me.

Keep your heart open, amor.
We need it from boys and men in this world.

Bet. I don't want to ever act tóxico again.

Busted Lip Circle

Paco says that Chava walked away
with a busted lip but other than that,
he was okay.

Except he isn't 'cause
Luisito's dad, Roy, took him home
to talk with Chava's dad.
Chava's dad yelled at Chava
and took away his phone right in front
of Luisito and Roy.

But Roy invited them
to join the Brothers Rising Circle.
He said we weren't
going to give up on Chava—
that he needed to learn
how to deal with his emotions
in a positive way.

Though Chava's dad
never said yes, he said
he would think about it.

I gotta admit,
I won't be looking forward
to seeing Chava there
but I guess all boys
need a chance to learn
better ways to feel and be.
Even Chava.

FaceChat Fumbles

Camelia FaceChats me.
I fumble for an apology
like a ball slipping
through my hands . . .

I'm sorry I was a knucklehead.

Camelia laughs, but says,

*Chivalry is dead, Elio, but I get it, you were trying
to be helpful in the worst possible way!
I'm giving you a pass.*

Thanks, Camelia.

You know what?

What?

*My mom found out about Chava sending my pics
around thanks to your mom.*

Ooh, sorry about that too.

No, no. It's good. My parents helped me break it off
with Chava. They even called his mom. And it's
worked! He's been avoiding me at school and
everything. It's honestly the biggest relief!

So does the school admin know?

No, not yet. I asked my parents not to tell them,
I don't want Chava to get in trouble.

But, Camelia, he needs to be held responsible
for what he did to you! He can't just get away with it!

I know, mansplainer! The truth is, I can't handle
going into a restorative circle with him,
which you know the school will do.
I'm just not ready for that yet.

I'm sure you probably know from Paco but Chava
and his dad are joining our Brothers Rising Circle.

Yeah, Paco told me they hope that'll stop him
from being such a butt wipe.

I'll have to see it to believe it.

Camelia.

Yes, Elio.

So, what do you need from me?

I just need you to be my friend, Elio.
Honestly, I don't know if I even like boys.
I just need to sit with all this for a while.

Sure thing. I'll be here even if I fumble.
Promise to let you call me out anytime.
In fact, I am apologizing in advance if I slip
back into knucklehead world, okay?

Ultraviolet Song

I approach my piano
after the call with my friend Camelia
and sit to stare at all the photos
of my family above it.
     Those who've loved.
     Those who've lost.
     Grandpops Mingo
     Grandmoms Maria
     magenta love
     gently flowing.

I place my hands on the keys
caress their smooth edges.
As I press, each key ignites
     with out-of-this-world color
     synchronizing with the song
     I can't help but compose now.

A song that is just for me—Elio Solis.

I am flushed with feelings
once trapped inside,
     now free.

They swish through my veins,
          circle my heart
                    pour into my hands,
                              come up to my vision,
          and I see:

     Pops's green face turning tender when he cries,
     Moms holding my hands in a cup of blue love,
     Rosie and Tita fluttering their sweet orange wings,
     my bros, Paco, Cheo, Luisito, and Raul,
     the council of dads,
     Fernando and Don Manuel,
     Mr. Trejo, and even Chava—
     all of them soul connections—
     dancing in a circle the color
     of golden fire around me.

Their music, my piano
          a resonant full sound
                    that fills the room
          and all of me.

Then I play an image
          with notes that whistle
                    and move,

and are born in new color.

It's our friend group
—Paco, Laurette, Camelia, and me—
      smiling and laughing
      in the green grassy
      quad of our school,
      red lips, indigo jeans,
      yellow-orange leaves,
      birds and bees
      flying all around us
      dipping into white clovers
      gorgeous colors
      bursting from my
      musical vision
      flooded in
      ultraviolet.

En lak ech
as deep and true
as my healing heart
was meant to feel.

Author's Note

Dear Readers,

Thank you for taking this ultraviolet ride with Elio. The idea for *Ultraviolet* came from my son, João, and his friend, Mario, who, after I'd written about a Latina girl's coming of age in *The Moon Within*, requested that I write one from a boy's perspective. They wanted to see a book that showed their inner lives and brought up conversations about puberty, first crushes, gender, and rites of passages—conversations that echoed who they were as cis Latino boys.

After some research, I soon discovered there are few fictional stories that address head-on how boys today deal emotionally with leaving childhood and entering adolescence. Few stories that help them navigate these new big feelings with tenderness and understanding. Most especially, brown and Black boys and other boys of color.

As I dug deeper into my research, I was shocked to find just how much we, as a patriarchal society—a society that favors men—have failed our boys emotionally. We don't allow them space to explore the tender parts of themselves—love, anger, rejection, grief, and hormonal confusion. They are raised to bury feelings—to be "macho" and "man up." We rarely provide safe spaces and ways for them to move through tough feelings or offer guidance on how to rise above them. It is a huge tragedy, really. When boys deny this very human part of themselves, it deeply impacts their relationships as they grow into men. And in that loss, in that wound, they sometimes treat others with the same hurt they feel or worse. Girls and women often bear the brunt of that wound, as we have seen by the violence in our society today. As a feminist and the mother of a boy, I want to offer boys examples of how they can find strength through nurturing their sensitivity and vulnerability.

Ultraviolet explores one boy's journey through the complicated landscape of falling in love and being heartbroken, through puberty and early adolescence as he tries to define his place in the world. But it is also about bigger topics like toxic masculinity, consent, and how we unconsciously or intentionally push patriarchal behavior. Because those in-between years (ages eleven to thirteen) are about exploration, it's important to have stories that help boys sort out complicated emotions and learn to respond in positive, loving, life-affirming, and healing ways. Only then can they fully embrace the beautiful complexity within them and carry that beauty with dignity, respect, and peace into the future.

With love and solidarity,
Aida

Acknowledgments

Many ultraviolet thanks to the spectacular Tracy Mack, my editor, whose brilliant insights and visions for this story gently nudged and inspired me to expand my creativity to produce a work of which I am so proud. Mil gracias, Leslie Owusu, for your great catches, consistent patience, and sweet encouragement along the way. Big shout-out to Kait Feldmann, who was the first editor to help me pull this story out of my brain and make me believe I could write a feminist book from a boy's perspective. I am grateful hasta la luna and back to my agent, aka my homegirl, Marietta Zacker, for never leading me astray with her perfect combination of honesty and love. The biggest agradecimiento to the incomparable Zeke Peña, who took my sweet Elio and created ultraviolet magic with this stunning cover illustration. Thank you, Marijka Kostiw, for your artistry in designing such a gorgeous book. A thousand thank-yous to the team at Scholastic who work hard behind the scenes in multiple ways to get our stories into readers' lives: Lizette Serrano, Emily Heddleson, Maisha Johnson, Sabrina Montenigro, Meredith Wardell, Jodie Cohen, Ellie Berger, Rachel Feld, Erin Berger, Seale Ballenger, Jarad Waxman, Jody Stigliano, Elizabeth Whiting, Jacqueline Rubin, Dan Moser, Roz Hilden, and Nikki Mutch. Special thanks to my publicists, Daniela Escobar and Amanda Trautmann, for really hustling for me. I appreciate you all and I am so grateful I get to work with you! I'm incredibly lucky to have a true friend in Dianna Perez, for thirty-three years and counting, who also happens to be a master story doctora. Her keen eyes, thoughtful questions, deep understanding of our culture and me, and what I am trying to do always guides my work—a million gracias, amiga mia!

Thank you to the Sun Ceremony Circle of boys and papás in my community—John and MJ, Cesar and Mario & Diego, Albert and Cheo, Rico and Jahziel, Roy and Dimas, Kieran and Zyan & Zarian—who created a space to untangle your hurts and rise above them, who found the sacred in your masculinity and came away gentler, nobler, and stronger souls for the benefit of us all. Thank you for teaching me and touching this story with your journey. Special thanks to Cesar Fernando Barragan and Brothers on the Rise for the phenomenal work to uplift BIPOC boys in Oakland. Thanks also to Luca, Tommy, Kali, Kingston, Dame Jr., Kahlil, Olu, Bilal, Ryan, and the boys at OSA who show fraternal love and understanding with emotional maturity beyond your years. Gen Z is doing it different! Many thanks to nurse Pam and Dr. Soifer in Cardiology at Children's Hospital for taking care of my son and for answering my many questions.

Gracias de todo corazón a mi amor, John, my children, Avelina and João, whose radiant love is what grounds me and makes me whole. This book could not have happened if I had not had the privilege to mother and pay witness to the miraculous blossoming of a young man. Gracias, my mi'jo, for humbling me, for making me laugh, and for sharing with me the wonder of your adolescence as you experienced it. Gracias, mi cielo azul, for inviting me into your ultraviolet heart and letting me listen to it beat with joy, break, and heal.

FONTS

The text of the book was set in 10.5 point Georgia. Georgia
is a serif typeface designed in 1993 by Matthew Carter and
is inspired by Scotch Roman designs of the 19th century.
The poem titles were set in Impact, a font designed by Geoffrey
Lee in 1965 and released by the Stephenson Blake foundry of
Sheffield. The author name was set in KG Shadow of the Day, a
handwritten font created by Kimberly Geswein in 2011.

AND MORE

The jacket art and title type were created by Zeke Peña.
The book was printed and bound at Grafica Veneta.
Production was overseen by Melissa Schirmer.
Manufacturing was supervised by Katie Wurtzel.
The book was designed by Marijka Kostiw
and edited by Tracy Mack.